MAKE WAY FOR MURDER

MAKE WAY FOR MURDER

A.A. MARCUS

WILDSIDE PRESS

MAKE WAY FOR MURDER

1

PETER HUNTER felt like an escaping convict, pinned against the wall by the prison searchlight.

High in the black sky glared a brilliant moon, its face squashed and misshapen. Its garish light struck the street with the harshness of a bomb flare.

A slim wiry man, Hunter leaned into the black building shadows, craned his neck up at the dark windows of the twelfth floor apartment across the street. The hush strung his nerves taut. Only a New York street, he thought, could be this quiet . . . its stillness accentuated by the memory of recent bustle.

He looked at the dark windows and swore softly. Because the lights should be on up there, Shackleford waiting for him.

His cold blue eyes swiveled up and down the street. He swore again. Through grated teeth, this time.

A uniformed policeman was sauntering toward him!

Hunter's eloquent hands stiffened. He shrank toward the wall. With intent casualness, the cop stopped to watch him.

Hunter turned his face away. Whistled with soft windy

discord. Took the white pack from his pocket, pretended to fumble for a cigarette.

The cop didn't move.

Hunter finally put a cigarette into his face. But didn't light it. *Couldn't* light it. Didn't dare spotlight his face for the law to remember.

And wondered why he felt this way. Why, it was as if he were about to commit a crime.

But the memory of what Shackleford had said was still strong. "If I'm not there, just come in and wait. The door will be open." Then, the little chuckle.

The nervous nasty chuckle . . .

Hunter's quick jittery fingers groped in his pockets, as if for a match. He watched the cop out of the corner of one eye.

The law elected to act helpful. Came forward with a lighter in its hand.

"Match?" The cop asked the question too solicitously. Suspicion bristled from him like spines from a porcupine.

"Thanks."

He flicked the sparking wheel. Sudden flame flared, distorted Hunter's thin face into a dissonant series of knife-edged planes and angles.

Hunter flinched. Klieg lights on his face. He bent to the flame and puffed. But turned half away, shielded his features behind a hunched shoulder.

The cop leaned forward insistently. He was going to see that face.

Hunter could feel the other's eyes now. Like twin Leica lenses, printing the image on a photographic plate in the brain.

He spewed forth a cloud of smoke. The cop coughed hard. Abruptly, the lighter flame snuffed out.

"Sorry," Hunter grunted.

The patrolman said nothing. He bounced the lighter in his hand for a moment, debating whether to start asking questions, then shrugged and turned away.

At a time like this, Hunter thought bitterly, you have to spend practically a weekend with the law.

At the end of the street, the cop turned to eye him again. Hunter took the bull by the horns, started toward him. The man in uniform turned the corner, disappeared.

Hunter turned his eyes back to the twelfth floor apartment. Still dark up there. He didn't like it. But his nerves wouldn't let him stall any longer. He had to do something.

He dragged deep, swallowed a cloud of smoke. The sensitive fingers snapped the cigarette into the gutter. It lay there, a single glowing eye, staring up at him. He walked toward the entrance of the apartment house he had been watching.

His tight lips formed soundless words. "God damn you, Munoz," they snarled.

The elevators were at the far end of the sumptuous foyer. A car was waiting at the ground floor, the inevitable handsome light-skinned Negro at the controls.

"Good evening, sir." The voice was like a well-modulated instrument, mellow and musical.

Hunter eyed him sympathetically. How many of them, he wondered, were there like this? Doing time in these cages while their agents tried to book recital dates . . . or sell that book . . . or find a gallery to show their work . . .

"A nice evening," he said softly, conscious of the inspection that was to decide whether he might be taken up, unannounced. He said, "Ten, please." His voice came out just as he wanted it to. Crisp and commanding.

It carried the day. The doors slid shut. The car shot skyward to the tenth floor.

He stepped out, again conscious of eyes on his back. Deliberately, he turned and met the stare of the elevator boy. The Negro flushed, suddenly aware that he was being rude. The doors hissed shut. The car plummeted back to earth.

Hunter thought: Another guy to remember you.

He took the fire stairs to the twelfth floor, exited and found himself standing in a wide, well-lighted, softly carpeted corridor. Soundlessly, he walked along it until he came to a door at the end of the hall marked: *Phineas T. Shackleford.*

He pressed the white button in the door jamb. Mellow chimes echoed within the apartment like cathedral bells. But after they died away, nothing happened.

He waited. He listened hard for a sound. Any sound.

Too damned quiet, he thought. His hands twitched. The stillness twanged his over-taut nerves. A deathly stillness that seemed to pervade the entire floor. Here there was no music from a too-loud radio. Not even trained-seal laughter at the antics of the television comics. The whole house seemed to be holding its breath, waiting for him to do a prat-fall.

He took a deep breath. He rang the bell. Again, the chimes. Again no answer.

He remembered what Shackleford had said . . . the nervous nasty chuckle. He turned the knob. The door swung open.

Hunter stood there, staring into blackness. He saw nothing, heard nothing.

He took the fire stairs to the twelfth floor, exited and He dredged the small flash from his pocket, shot its thin pencil beam around the room. Still nothing . . .

His hands clenched. His lips tightened. He stepped inside. One pace he went, then the sudden sense of danger shot through him like a bolt of lightning. He threw himself to the side.

A sharp tearing sound as if something had caught his sleeve. A snap—then sudden light. He turned toward the source of the blow.

He blinked against the onslaught of brightness, faced his adversary in shocked surprise.

A Chinese!

Hunter backed away. The Chinese came toward him. The man's hand moved and something glinted in it.

A knife!

And, even as he saw the ugly weapon, he felt something at his back. He put one hand out, felt the wall behind him. He had retreated as far as he could.

The Chinese crouched, stalked Hunter like a jungle cat, poised to pounce. His eyes glowed yellow. Hate hammered the flat planes of his face into grim implacability.

Hunter's eyes were on the knife. The hand that gripped it held the blade low, ready for the uppercutting slash. No chance to wrest it away. But instinctively Hunter acted. His slim wiry body arched through the air in a feet-first leap. One shoe caught the attacker a glancing blow on the jaw. The Chinese staggered under the impact.

Hunter scrambled to his feet, clutched the knife-hand with his own quick left. The Chinese threshed wildly to free himself. Hunter pounded his free right fist to the other's belly. Breath exploded in a *whoosh*.

The blow should have slowed the Chinese down. Instead, he struggled more furiously to free himself. Hunter felt his hold on the deadly knife-hand slipping. Again, he flailed upward with his right fist. It thudded against the other's eye. The knife-fighter screamed out, writhed in pain and, convulsively, tore free.

The suddenness of release made him stumble. Hunter charged after him, put all his strength into a long overhand right swing. It landed hard on the jaw.

The Chinese staggered back, slid onto the seat of his pants. Hunter kicked the hand that held the knife. The weapon clattered against the wall. The prostrate man grabbed at Hunter's foot. The foot pulled away, then moved in again, swinging. The shoe cracked against the fallen man's head.

He collapsed, head thumping the carpeted floor. A trickle of blood began a meandering journey along his temple, then down the side of his face. He lay still.

Hunter snatched up the knife. His vibrant hands touched it as though they were exploring a writhing rattlesnake. One sensitive finger tested the finely honed point, recoiled from it.

Suddenly Hunter shivered, stiffened into alertness. Had the figure on the floor moved?

He approached it warily, knife held ready to strike. Except for the shallow breathing of unconsciousness, the body seemed absolutely still.

Hunter's face set. He bent, opened one of the shadowed eyelids. Sightlessly, the bared eye stared up at him. He pointed the tip of the knife at the empty pupil. Inexorably, the deadly point descended until it seemed it must pierce the unprotected organ.

The eye never moved: the pupil continued to stare; without contraction, without dilation. Finally, Hunter nodded, convinced. He released his hold on the eyelid. It oozed shut.

Hunter rose. Abruptly, his knees began to tremble. He swayed, almost fell. His stomach tightened until he felt he must retch. He stumbled to the door, leaned his head against it.

It suddenly dawned on him that he'd been in a fight for his life—and had almost lost.

He couldn't stay any longer. He swung the door open and took a step out into the hall, then he realized he still held the knife. He turned back.

The figure lay supine on the floor. Even in unconsciousness, those features still held their malignantly tigerish cast.

Hunter tossed the knife back. The blade glinted as it described a lazy little loop, then fell point first and hit the carpeted floor with a little dull thump. Hilt quivering, it stuck there, beside the still body.

Hunter stood, swaying slightly, half-hypnotized by the oscillating motion. Seeing, in his mind's eye, that malevolent blade piercing deep into his flesh . . . that evil hilt protruding from his heart . . . quivering . . .

He shuddered, literally tore himself away. The sound of the door slamming shut was the happiest noise he had heard all night.

2

THE TELEPHONE was clanging like a firehouse bell when Hunter arrived home. He glared at it until, after pealing a dozen times, it fell silent.

He stood in the doorway a moment then, like a man counting his blessings, he began a slow circuit of the walls of his living room. His hands fingered the albums of records in their custom-built racks, lingered lovingly on the backs of the books.

Slowly, the tense face relaxed. He opened a cabinet door, took out a bottle and poured himself four ounces of scotch. The phone began again just as he raised the glass to his lips.

He ignored it, but waited until its clamor had stopped. Then he downed the drink in one long gulp. Color rushed back into his pale face, tinted the tightly stretched skin at the high cheekbones.

His eyes fell to the long slash in his sleeve, put there by the Chinese's first blow, the one he'd barely escaped in the dark. Involuntarily, he shuddered, then poured another stiff drink and downed it.

He went into the immaculate kitchenette. The deft

hands busied themselves, slicing rye bread neatly, adding ham and cheese. He poured out a glass of milk, put the sandwich and glass on a tray and took them back into the living room. While he was eating, the telephone renewed its impatient clamor.

Hunter hesitated, reluctantly put down the half-eaten sandwich. He picked up the receiver. "Hello . . ."

"Señor Hunter?" It was Munoz.

At the sound of his client's voice, Hunter's lips tightened. He said, "Yes?" guardedly.

"Señor Munoz is here." Hunter was momentarily aware of a sense of pain behind the man's voice. "I bid you good evening, Señor Hunter."

"What's good about it?" Hunter asked flatly.

"The news you have for me, I hope. You were at Señor Shackleford's apartment tonight?"

"Yes."

"And you conferred with him, señor?"

"No."

"Ay!" The sound came out half sigh, half groan. "May I ask why not?"

"He wasn't there."

"Not there, señor?"

"But the door was open. I walked in."

"Walked in?"

"You were paying me to see Shackleford, weren't you?" Hunter asked pugnaciously.

"I do not understand."

"Neither do I. I was attacked—"

"*Attacked?*"

"Attacked. Damn near skinned alive."

16

"If I may ask you, señor—by whom?"

"How the hell should I know? And I didn't wait around to ask questions."

"You must tell me more, señor." Munoz's pain was unmistakable now. "It is important that—"

"Listen, Munoz," Hunter cut in savagely. "You paid me to call a guy named Shackleford, whom I'd never heard of or seen, to negotiate about getting back something you said belonged to you. I did that. I arranged to meet him. I tried to see him. You got what you paid for with your lousy two hundred. Now, I quit."

Munoz groaned. "But you must—"

"Like hell I must." Hunter slammed the receiver down, yet sat there waiting for the phone to ring again.

It took less than a minute. He picked it up. Irritatedly, he said, "Go away."

"I must know more, Señor Hunter." The pain came through stronger now, the torment more apparent in the way the words were bitten off.

"I told you—you got what you paid for."

"But you do not understand." Urgency conquered the pain in the Spaniard's voice. The words came in a torrent. "If they have reached New York . . . if they are so close . . . I *must* know, señor . . ."

"*They?* Who in hell are *they?*"

Munoz began again, like the needle caught in the groove of the broken record. "It is a matter of extreme urgency—"

"Not to me, it isn't." Hunter broke off.

When the phone rang still again, he picked it up, said wearily, "Oh, go to hell," and put it down again.

17

It didn't ring any more.

He took a record from one of the albums and put it on the built-in player. The soothing devotions of Cesar Franck's *Symphonic Variations* poured out. He stood, listening, eyes closed, almost as if the music were an opiate calming him, then walked to the window and looked out. The bright misshapen moon that had so disturbed him earlier still rained down its light.

After a few minutes, a long sleek Cadillac slid up to the curb. The tall and usually aristocratic-looking figure of Eduardo Munoz emerged from behind the wheel.

Only, even from where Hunter sat, five stories skyward, the figure of the Latin looked anything but aristocratic at the moment. Hunched over tautly, the man wove an unsteady, jagged path across the sidewalk to the entrance. It took him an inordinately long time to make his way upstairs. So very long that Hunter decided his visitor had changed his mind. But no— eventually the doorbell rang.

Hunter opened the door and the man on the outside almost fell through. The Spaniard brushed away the quick hand that reached out to steady him.

"No, no," he muttered. "Is all right. I shall manage myself." He staggered to the sofa. He sat down heavily, as if his body were a burden too overwhelming to be borne any longer.

He kept his coat buttoned up tight to the neck. When Hunter offered to relieve him of it, Munoz waved him away. Hunter shrugged, sat down opposite his visitor.

The man seemed to have aged twenty-five years since morning. The face, so handsome and aristocratic twelve

18

hours ago, was gaunt and drawn now. There were deep, acid-etched lines around the mouth. Body hunched over, Munoz sat with his arms across his chest. He kept them folded tightly, as if he feared that if he let them drop to his sides, his body would fall apart.

With visible effort, the Spaniard lifted his head. The skin was stretched so tight across his face it seemed transparent. Hunter found himself staring into pain-drenched eyes.

"It is imperative," Munoz began, painfully biting off the words behind tight lips, "that you inform me of what has transpired."

Instead of answering, Hunter waved the bottle at him. "You need a drink," he said.

Munoz shook his head. He fought on doggedly. "You procrastinate, señor. You put me off. But the time is short. And I must know. Quickly."

"You got what you paid for, Munoz."

"If it is money you want—"

"It is. After what I went through tonight—"

"Money!" The Spaniard spat the word out contemptuously. Little white moons appeared in the pale surface of his lower lip as his teeth furrowed it. He tossed a black pinseal wallet into Hunter's lap, sucked his breath sharply at the pain which, apparently, even this little effort caused him.

"There is money, Hunter. Take whatever you wish."

Hunter looked inside. There was a packet of bills in an inner compartment. Crisp green hundred-dollar treasury notes.

He flushed. How do you put a price on risking your

life? Finally, he shrugged, counted out five notes and put them into his pocket.

He said, "All right, ask your questions."

"*Bueno.*" The sarcasm was bitter. Then: "At Señor Shackleford's—you met someone?"

"Yes."

"Describe him, señor," he hesitated, then added, "or her."

"Him. A Chinese."

"A Chinese?"

"He was waiting for me, with a knife. Shackleford laid a trap."

Munoz's head sank to his chest. He muttered to himself in rapid incoherent Spanish. He looked up, after a moment, with great effort.

"So, señor," the breath he drew seemed like a sword in his side, "they have come to do battle. Good. But they will not prevail. I, Munoz, will triumph."

He gestured grandiloquently, carried away. The palms of his hands came away from the jacket, turned upward. They were wet—with brilliant crimson.

Hunter leaped as though shot. "Good God, man—"

Munoz rose, backed away from him. His face contorted. He shook himself convulsively, like a bull fighting to pin down the maddening *muleta.*

Hunter grasped his shoulders to steady him. Munoz struck the detective's hands away, savagely. He leaned against the arm of the sofa. Lips locked tight against his torment, he fought to stay erect.

He turned burning eyes on Hunter. "They have come," he said. "They are *here.*"

His skin was the raw gray of fresh clay. Hunter stood by, to catch him when he fell.

"But they will fail. They *must* fail."

A fine froth foamed to his lips. A cough racked his body; the froth became a needle spray of tiny glittering red droplets. He clutched hard at his belly.

"*La calavera*," he cried suddenly. The words wrenched their way out of his tortured guts. "*La calavera de plata.*"

He staggered, almost fell, snatched at the arm of the sofa again, caught it, stood swaying like a reed in a hurricane.

"Señor," the tormented burning eyes rested on Hunter again, "it is ours. My country's. Mine." The next words were cut off by a convulsion of crimson-flecked coughing.

Then suddenly, the paroxysm ended. There was a moment of lucidity. His eyes cleared. He drew himself straight as a sword. He said, very distinctly, "*La calavera de plata.*"

Abruptly, the wire-taut nerves slackened. The tensed straining muscles dissolved into flaccid flesh. He pitched forward, hit the floor face first with an empty hollow thump.

Hunter didn't move. His eyes, soft and pitying, rested on the body, now so still. It was all over now, he knew.

Only death could be so calm . . .

He sat down slowly. The expressive fingers rubbed together, worried one another. The room was so quiet he could hear himself breathing . . .

He shook his head to break the spell. He had a body on his hands, a body he had to get rid of. How would he do it?

21

He went to the window, looked down at Munoz's Cadillac. If he took the body around to the side of the building . . . and carried it down the service stairs . . . then drove it off and left it somewhere . . .

He nodded in decision, bent to the corpse to find the keys. As he did so, a disquieting thought struck him.

La calavera de plata—what the hell was that?

3

HE SAT AT the wide mahogany desk in his office the following day, tired and mystified. The soft green of the decor soothed him not at all. The sumptuous leather that he rested on did not relax him.

He was tired because he had slept badly the night before. And he was mystified because there was not one single word in the morning papers about the discovery of the body of his late client, Eduardo Munoz.

What the hell kind of reporters did the papers have nowadays? Was it no longer news when a well-dressed corpse was found in a Cadillac parked on a fashionable East Side street? Irritably, he shook his head. He knew perfectly well the cops had picked up the car. He'd waited around until he'd seen them do so. So, surely, the newspapers would have gotten the tip.

The buzzer beneath his desk rasped, interrupting his thoughts. There was a visitor waiting in the outer office. His quick finger jabbed at a button, releasing the catch on the communicating door.

A woman entered, and a single thought flashed through his mind.

Exquisite!

She was a Chinese, and even tinier than the tiny variety of Chinese. South China, maybe Canton, he thought. The Northerners grew pretty tall. But she was perfection in miniature. Her carriage was queenly. She moved toward him as if the world were at her feet. Pride and dignity reflected themselves in every aspect of her face.

He rose. She said, "Mr. Hunter?"

Her voice was a delightful thing, soft and glowing, with a faint hint of distant music in it. An Oriental music, muted and melodious . . . like distant temple bells chiming on the side of a mountain.

He nodded to her question, led her to the chair beside his desk. As she walked toward it, he was gradually aware of a whispering that accompanied her movement. It was an intriguing sound, a sound that piqued his curiosity because obviously it must emanate from something she wore. And yet—it couldn't come from that neat, severely cut, black woolen dress.

No, that seductive whisper must come from something underneath what he could see of her clothing.

Cut it out, he growled soundlessly to himself. Acting like a prep school boy at his first dance.

But the question persisted: what feminine undergarment would cause that provocative rustle?

In his mind's eye, he saw it . . . a bright shocking scarlet . . . daringly cut . . .

To himself, he grinned.

But his wary eyes never left her body as she seated herself. He was searching for the bright flash of color beneath the dress . . . the source of that intriguing sound. Still, the way she sat was too demure, too purely femfully at slimly tapered ankles. The tiny feet were modishly shod in simple black suede shoes.

Suddenly conscious that she was studying his face, he looked up. The sudden rush of heat to his cheeks amazed and irritated him.

What the hell's happening to you, Hunter?

He found himself looking into her eyes. They were like ocean water suffused with sunlight—a sparkling green.

She said, simply, "Mr. Hunter, I am in very great trouble."

Looking again, he could now see the shadows lurking in the depths of those ocean-green eyes. And he could hear the distress in that melodious voice.

He said, forcing himself to sound completely businesslike: "Tell me about your trouble. Maybe I can help you, Miss . . ."

"Toy," she said. "Juanita Toy."

Juanita—the Spanish name was totally unexpected.

The astonishment in his face amused her. For a moment, her sad-eyed gravity was broken by a dazzling smile that was sheer dancing sunlight.

"My name surprises you, Mr. Hunter?"

"Miss Toy," he assured her brusquely, "my business is people. Nothing surprises me."

"I would not care for such a business," she said thoughtfully.

"We cannot all do what we like."

"True," she said, and fell into silence.

Again, he studied her. She was young, perhaps in her

early twenties. There was a purity in her face that compelled his interest. It seemed to have been carved from jade, so cleanly designed were its planes and angles.

He said, finally, "And your business, Miss Toy?"

She sighed. "I have been wondering how to begin. Perhaps I should explain that I am not an American."

"I had gathered that."

Her smile was rueful. "My speech—"

"Makes English sound so much better."

Delight glanced in the sea-green eyes. She inclined her head gracefully.

"Just where are you from, Miss Toy?"

"I was born in a small country in Central America whose name I prefer not to mention. My father had been one of that group of Chinese scholars who felt themselves superior to the tangled politics of their country . . . who made the mistake of being indifferent to Dr. Sun Yat Sen's dream of a strong, united China. When Dr. Sun succeeded in realizing his ambition, he stooped to wreak vengeance on those who had ignored him. To escape, my father fled to the New World. There, he found the woman who became his wife and my mother."

"Hence," Hunter said, "the Juanita."

"Exactly." The tiny Chinese frowned prettily. "Although I wonder now why I tell you so much of myself."

"I'm glad you do, nevertheless."

She said, "Thank you," in a tone that was almost imperious.

His sensitive fingers drummed on the desk. He said, "She must be very beautiful, your mother."

"She was very beautiful."

The words were uttered sadly and, after they had died away, an unvoiced echo remained. As music lingers with the hearer after it has ended.

Hunter said, quickly, "I'm sorry."

She said nothing. There was a long moment of quiet melancholy.

Her face, in repose, revealed the Latin heritage of her mother. It was there in the faint tint of olive in the flawless skin, the enigmatic shadows that enhanced the brilliance of the emerald eyes. He had the feeling—and how he got it he couldn't tell—that bright passion smoldered beneath that facade of serenity.

She started, as though from a reverie. Consciously, she set herself to meet his searching gaze. It was as if she had shamed herself by betraying her inner emotion to a stranger.

She said, very crisply, "I came here to get help for Ramon, Mr. Hunter—not to discuss my ancestral antecedents."

"Ramon?"

"My brother."

"And what can I do for Ramon?"

"Find him."

"He's missing?"

"Yes."

"How long?"

"Since arriving in New York. Two weeks now."

"And you came here to find him?"

Her hesitation was so momentary as to be almost imperceptible.

She said, "Partly."

27

He waited for her to complete her answer. She added nothing. Finally, he said, almost dismissively, "Two weeks aren't such a long time, Miss Toy."

Again, she remained silent.

"Especially," he went on, "when you're sure nothing has happened to him."

A frown furrowed the pure expanse of her brow. Like sentries on duty, shadows marched into her eyes. "How do you know that, Mr. Hunter?" she asked.

"Quite obvious. If he were in danger, you could scarcely have endured two weeks of doubt and ignorance as to his whereabouts. Therefore, you know he is safe."

"You are shrewd, Mr. Hunter."

"Not shrewd, Miss Toy. It's just that I've seen people who were concerned about their loved ones. They did not have your—equanimity."

His penetration of her mind disturbed her. She said, "I hardly know how to answer you."

He leaned forward. The perfume she wore reached his nostrils faintly, a dry, intriguing scent. He touched one finger lightly to the sleeve of her dress.

"Just exactly what is it you are concerned about, Miss Toy?"

Her gaze fell to his hand, then lifted. Her green eyes met his ice-blue ones, measured them. Eventually she said, almost as if making a confession, "I am afraid that Ramon will kill someone, Mr. Hunter."

If she expected him to be shocked, she was disappointed. His face remained impassive. "And you want me to stop him?"

"Yes. Find him and stop him."

He said, softly, "You'll have to tell me more."

She sighed. "I had hoped not to tell you as much as I already have."

He opened the eloquent hands in a gesture that was half apology.

"Still," she said, "I can see that I must explain."

He waited.

She rose from the chair, a flowing rhythmic motion. For a moment, it seemed she was about to leave. Instead, she turned to face him.

She said, "I must collect my thoughts, Mr. Hunter."

Still, he said nothing.

She began to pace the office, her stride crisp, yet measured. Intently, he watched her, his ice-blue eyes taking in every detail: the straight square-shouldered way she carried the tiny queenly body; the lithe movement of the slim legs; the proud lift of the perfectly proportioned breasts . . .

And, with his mind as much as with his ears, he could again hear that seductive rustle of whatever it was she wore beneath that dress. The sound kindled to a slow fire deep inside him.

With unhurried quickness, she sat again. "I really must tell you everything, I'm afraid." A shy regret underscored the music in her glowing voice.

"I'm afraid so."

"After all, one cannot go to the police and ask them to stop one's brother from committing murder, can one?"

"Obviously not."

"Because if they should fail to stop him . . . If he *should* kill . . ."

He finished the thought for her. "Then the police would know where to look for their murderer."

"Exactly."

"Tell me the rest."

"How shall I begin?" she asked. She put her ungloved hand on the desk while she sought the right words.

He studied the fingers. They were well-formed, square, and they looked capable. Long without seeming elongated. And calm. They made him aware of the excited tenseness of his own hands.

He said, abruptly, "Why should Ramon want to commit murder?"

"It is on my account."

"Tell me about it."

"Very well," she conceded. "You see, Mr. Hunter, I was about to be married to Ricardo De Sola, the son of the premier and . . . well, dictator, you would say . . . of our country. A certain gentleman stopped the marriage."

"How? And why?"

"How? By advising the premier that the United States would frown on the union of a Caucasian and an Oriental at so high a level." Though wryness entered her voice, no sign of bitterness marred the dispassionate calm of the finely carved features. "Why did this gentleman say this? Perhaps because it suited his own political purposes. Perhaps because he knew I would exert my influence to end his exploitation of my adopted people."

"And so your prospective father-in-law, the dictator, forbade the marriage?"

"Yes." Her sigh caused the exquisitely shaped breasts to lift.

He watched, and waited.

"Whereupon I ran away to your New York in a melo-dramatic attempt to forget."

"Hardly sensible."

"In matters of the emotions, Mr. Hunter, we rarely stop to be sensible."

"I wouldn't know, Miss Toy," he said dryly. "I avoid emotionalism. Your brother came with you?"

"Yes." She ignored the rebuke. "And the *gentleman*," here an astringent sarcasm bit into the word, "who, to use a melodramatic phrase, ruined my life, followed soon after."

"Why?"

"Because, quite accidentally, I have acquired certain documents which prove him to be somewhat less than a sincere friend to our premier."

"And now he wants them back?"

"He offers great sums of money for them."

"You refuse?"

"Naturally."

"But you haven't used the incriminating documents against him yet?"

"No."

"Why not?"

Remote and inscrutable, the lovely green eyes took on an emerald hardness. "Because he suffers more while waiting for me to do so."

"Cat and mouse," he suggested.

"A feminine trait." She shrugged . . . a graceful gesture . . . then said, "You will help me with Ramon?"

He opened his hands in a movement meant to convey

helplessness. "It's impossible, I'm afraid."

Consternation seamed her lovely face. "But why?"

"Because when a grown man decides to commit murder, Miss Toy—and is willing to risk the consequences—nothing short of imprisonment or death can stop him."

Her hand reached out in an impulsively pleading gesture. "But you will *try* to stop him, Mr. Hunter? At least, you will try?"

"If you want me to." He inclined his head. "But remember—no guarantees."

Hurriedly, as though she feared he might change his mind, she opened the smart suede bag and took out a black lizard-skinned wallet. She counted out bank notes, spread them on the desk.

His eyes narrowed. They were hundred-dollar bills. Five crisp green hundreds.

Just like Munoz, he thought. His hands stiffened. His lips ironed down into a tight thin line.

He thought, brusquely: *Centuries. Everybody shoves centuries at you nowadays. More trouble.*

She was saying, "Will this be enough, Mr. Hunter?"

Resentment made him answer, sharply, "For a while."

She said, "There will be more if it is necessary."

He thought: I don't doubt it.

And now it was Hunter's turn to pace the floor. She watched with quiet detachment, perfectly willing to wait until he had something to say.

He turned to her. "Where will I find your brother?"

She started to say, "But I don't—"

He cut in sharply. "Yes, you do. Or at least you know where to start looking."

Again, admiration glowed in the sea-green eyes. She said, "He is very much attached to a man named Phineas Shackleford."

Somehow, he controlled his face. But the telltale hands jerked as if some impatient puppeteer had snatched at their strings.

"Shackleford." He repeated the name softly, yet with great intensity.

"You know him?"

He tried to smile with lips stiff as concrete. "It is an odd name," he said.

Her eyes searched his face. To avoid them, he turned to the window, pretended to look out. With his back to her, he asked, "And who is the man you fear your brother may kill?"

"A certain Eduardo Munoz."

Munoz!

It was like a blow to the pit of the stomach. A chill of fear iced his spine. Like the pumping of a frightened heart, the hands clenched and unclenched themselves.

But, when he turned from the window to face her, his face was impassive. Deliberately, he went back behind the desk and began to ask routine questions, the answers to which he carefully noted on a desk pad.

Where was she staying? And where could he find Mr. Shackleford? And did she know the whereabouts of Eduardo Munoz?

Knowing only too well the answer to that last question.

And finally: "Do you have a snapshot of your brother, Miss Toy—so that I'll know him when I find him?"

"I thought you might ask that. I brought one along."

She reached into the chic bag, produced a small envelope. She handed it to him. He opened it, looked at the small photograph. He had to close his eyes.

Steady, Hunter, steady!

The dread he had felt a moment before at the mention of Munoz's name went crawling up and down his spine again like a hairy-footed centipede. Somehow, he controlled himself. Somehow, he forced himself to look again at the photo.

It hadn't changed. It was still the Chinese who had tried so hard to cut him to shreds in Shackleford's apartment last night.

He heard her ask, the sound coming from a great distance, "Will there be anything else, Mr. Hunter?"

And a voice he hardly recognized as his own replied crisply, "Nothing, Miss Toy. Nothing else. I'll go right to work on it."

"And you will let me know how you progress?"

"As soon as there is any progress, Miss Toy."

She extended her ungloved hand. He took it, found himself holding it too tightly, too long, before he released it. As he accompanied her to the door, he was again conscious of the faint seductive susurration emanating from whatever it was she was wearing beneath the black dress.

This time, though, he didn't dwell on it. There were too many other wild thoughts fighting for possession of his mind.

He opened the door. She said, gravely, "Goodbye, Mr. Hunter. I feel better now. Much better."

"I'm glad."

"I'm sure Ramon is in good hands."

She was out in the hall. A sudden wild impulse seized him. He said, sharply, "Miss Toy."

She turned, surprise in her eyes.

"Miss Toy," he repeated, "what is the meaning of the words—*la calavera de plata?*"

His eyes probed her face. Was she taken aback? He couldn't be sure, her surprise had been so momentary— if it had existed at all.

Her smile was radiant. "How mysterious, Mr. Hunter. Those words simply mean—*the silver skull.*"

He stood in the open doorway, watching the smooth rustling grace of that exquisite figure as it made its way to the elevators. A car arrived, she flashed him her dazzlingly sunlit smile, the doors slid shut. She was gone.

And Peter Hunter had a feeling that something inside him was going with her.

4

LIKE A PANTHER leashed to a stake, Peter Hunter prowled the perimeter of his office. The questing hands rubbed against each other as though a fabric was passing between them, to be analyzed for flaws. His sharp face had corkscrewed into a puzzled grimace.

A simple problem Juanita Toy had given him: Keep my brother from killing a man.

But the man was dead already.

Her brother, then, could have been the killer.

Another thing: *La calavera de plata*—the silver skull —what did that signify? Where did it fit in?

Names kept swimming into his thoughts, then out again, like ameba moving through the field of a microscope.

Munoz . . . Ramon . . . Shackleford . . . Juanita Toy . . .

He shook his head. The room was still alive with her presence. Her perfume yet hung in the air, faint and dry and provocative.

He went back to his desk, sat down. The crisp hundred-dollar bills still lay there, staring up at him.

He thought: *Come on, Hunter, pick them up. They can't hurt you. They're only money.*

Reluctantly, he reached for them. But the lean mercurial fingers, exerting a will of their own, shied away.

At that moment, the buzzer sounded. He had a visitor. Hunter shrugged, swept up the banknotes, thrust them into his pocket. That done, he pressed the button that unlocked the communicating door.

His caller burst into the room as though rocket-propelled. He strode across the floor and planted himself six feet from the desk, legs spread wide, chest stuck out. And his hand, when it came out of the deep pocket of his coat, pointed an automatic at Hunter's navel.

"Where is it?" the visitor demanded harshly.

Hunter's cold blue eyes narrowed, fixed on the weapon momentarily, then swept up to examine the man who held it.

He saw a tall figure, thin and undulating as an eel, swathed in a black coat long enough to be a shroud. His hat was black, too, and broad-brimmed, draping his face in mourning. The skin was the yellow of prolonged exposure to the tropical sun. And the eyes, shadowed beneath the hat's funereal brim, burned with a dark fire.

Hunter said, "Put the gun away."

"When you tell me where it is."

"Where what is?"

"You know what I'm referring to." The man in the black hat jutted his chin forward. His jaw tapered like a grave-digger's spade. His voice grated—as if the spade were scratching rock.

Hunter said, wearily, "You're stupid."

37

Bushy black eyebrows climbed up Black Hat's forehead.

"Because," he went on, "you're pointing a gun you don't intend to use."

"Eh? Why not?"

"You want me to tell you something. I can't if I'm dead."

The fiery dark eyes swiveled from Hunter's face to the weapon. He laughed softly—a nervous nasty chuckle.

"They said you were clever." Mirth twisted his long lips. "And you are."

Hunter frowned. The voice had a familiar ring. Yet, he could not place it. His eyes narrowed as the hand that held the gun pointed its barrel upward toward the ceiling.

"But," the harsh voice went on to say, "by the same token, you must know I won't be put off. You possess it. I desire it. And—I have the artillery to gain my point."

Hunter's eyes remained riveted on the weapon. Like panthers tensing for a spring, his hands locked themselves into half fists on the desk.

He said, "I don't know what the hell you're talking about."

"Poppycock! Don't evade me, sir. It's here—you haven't had time to dispose of it."

Hunter frowned. Where had he heard that voice before?

"I won't be put off, sir. If necessary I shall search these premises at gunpoint." He looked around the room and pointed dramatically with his free left hand at files and closet. "There . . . and there . . ."

It was a flamboyant gesture, compelling in its intensity. Hunter's eyes followed the pointing finger. As soon as they did, he knew he'd committed a fatal error.

Desperately he tried to recover, to shield his head with his arm, to twist away from the blow.

Too late.

The black-coated man's fist plummeted down. Sunlight glinted on the barrel of the automatic. It cracked against the side of Hunter's head. The impact knocked him out of the chair and down to his knees.

Red mist spurted into his brain, suffocating him, blotting out consciousness. Frantically, he fought it, pushing hard against the overwhelming weight with fingers of clay. Grimly, he began to lift himself.

His fingers scratched on the side of the desk, reached its edge. He began to pull himself erect. But just as his knees lifted clear of the floor, a second thunderclap exploded.

The red mist descended in clouds now. It turned into blackness. He felt himself sinking . . . sinking . . .

Time immemorial passed. The mist turned from black to red again. He didn't know where he was—nor who he was—but he knew he was alive again.

He knew that because he could hear a noise.

It was a nice cruel noise. It hurt his ears. It sounded and felt like a hacksaw ripping raucously across the top of his skull.

But, because of it, he knew he was alive.

He shook his head—and wished he hadn't. The movement brought the red mist into his brain again.

He fought the inclination to retch. After a doubtful moment, it passed.

The red mist softened into pink now. He saw things. Things he knew: his desk; his file cabinets.

And the noise—he could identify it now. It was a telephone. A ringing telephone.

His hands reached high, found the edge of the desk. Like a mountain climber, suspended above the peril of on abyss, he pulled his body up.

He stood swaying. It was a great victory. Exhausted, he flopped into his chair.

The blue eyes, filmed and cloudy now, swept the room. It was empty. His assailant had gone.

He picked up the telephone. "Hello," he said. His voice echoed and re-echoed within his skull, like a metal ball ricochetting between tin walls.

"Mr. Hunter," a voice asked anxiously, "is it you?"

As suddenly as the snap of fingers, he was wide awake.

"Mr. Hunter." The voice was alarmed. *"Mr. Hunter!"*

He said, crisply, "Just a minute, Miss Toy." He laid the phone down gently and went to the water cooler in the corner.

He put his head directly beneath the tap, letting the ice-cold water stream through his hair. It felt like an ice-pick chopping at the top of his skull. He shook his head, scattering droplets like a retriever emerging from the river. He dried his hair on his handkerchief and returned to the phone.

"Yes, Miss Toy," he said, all business, "what is it?"

"Are you all right?"

He couldn't answer immediately. Two contradictory thoughts were fighting for control of his brain.

First, there was the voice itself, clouded with anxiety, yet full of music. Little more than a whisper it was, but alive with bright little tinkling bells.

But, on the other hand—why had she called? Why should she think there was something wrong?

Had she known he was to be attacked?

"Mr. Hunter—please answer me."

Now, he could take no pleasure in the apparent concern for his safety. The conviction was too strong that there must assuredly be a connection between her visit and his grief.

He said, "Believe me, Miss Toy, I feel swell. Perfectly swell."

"But you sound strange."

"It's my head."

"Your head?"

"It's sometimes weak."

"I begin to think so." She became businesslike. "I called to inform you that I shall be having dinner with Mr. Shackleford tonight at the Garland Hotel."

He thought: Is that *really* why you called? He said, "Yes?"

"I thought you would like to know."

"I would? Why?"

"It will give you a chance to see Mr. Shackleford and, through him, to reach Ramon."

"Swell, Miss Toy. I'll join you there. What time?"

"Oh, no," she said quickly, "you must not."

41

"Why not?"

"Ramon must not know, Mr. Hunter. He would never forgive me if he knew what I have done."

"*Done*, Miss Toy? What have you done, exactly?"

"Set someone to watch him. He would be furious."

"Oh," he said.

"So, you will come to the Garland, but not join me."

He started to answer, then checked himself. A sudden light had shone in his brain. He put his hand to the side of his head, felt the bruise there. He winced.

He said, "It won't be necessary, Miss Toy."

"Then how will you know him?" She sounded baffled.

"Know whom?" There was a teasing light in his eyes.

"Mr. Shackleford."

He touched the bruise again. A picture formed in his mind—the image of a tall eel-like man with dark burning eyes, swathed in funereal black.

He said, "Don't worry, Miss Toy—I'll know Mr. Shackleford when I see him."

And hung up before she could answer.

5

THE VOICE from the doorway was like a low genial rumble of thunder. It said, "That's quite a bruise you got on your noggin, boy."

Peter Hunter straightened up from the task of restoring to order the mess that Phineas Shackleford had made in his search.

He said, "How the hell did you get here, Grogan?"

Inspector Grogan laughed and the rumble of thunder deepened.

"The door was open. I walked in."

Hunter said, sharply, "Well, you're here now. Shut the door behind you and walk in."

Inspector Grogan complied. He was a veritable mountain of a man, his head a huge rock, his body a vast boulder—the two joined together without benefit of neck. You had the feeling that, beneath his collar, there was a neatly troweled layer of cement where head and shoulders met.

"What brings you here, Grogan?"

Grogan smiled genially. "I got questions for you. Interesting questions."

"Such as?"

"Munoz." He thrust his big head forward. His eyes were an inert gray-black, the color of asphalt. They narrowed now, fixed on Hunter's face.

Hunter said: "What's Munoz?"

"A man. Know him?"

"Should I?"

"He was a client, wasn't he?"

"Was he?"

Grogan eased his huge body into a chair, a slow ponderous movement. "Playin' games, hey?"

Hunter said nothing.

Grogan's big head swiveled like the ball turret of a Sherman tank as his eyes swept the room. His tone hardened as he asked, "You operate under a private detective's license, right?"

Hunter nodded. His hands stiffened as if bracing to meet a shock.

"And you'd like to keep it, wouldn't you, Hunter?"

Hunter's quick fingers tightened. His angry lips spat words like a machine gun spits bullets. "Don't play the heavy cop with me, Grogan. If you want my ticket, try to take it away—if you think you can make the action stand up in court."

Instead of being angry, Grogan's big face creased into a smile.

"Like to hear you get sore, boy."

"And if you want information from me, don't go teasing for it like a coy little whore, Grogan. Ask for it like a man."

Grogan's smile vanished. His face was stiff as mortar.

44

He lifted the gray-black eyes as he said, softly, "Watch your tongue, boy."

Hunter brushed the admonition away with a careless wave of his hand.

"I talk too much," he admitted.

Grogan sighed, said, "Let's start over."

"Let's."

"You know this Munoz?"

"I know him."

"A dark, good-looking, Spanish-type guy?"

"That's him."

"How well d'you know him, Hunter? Have you got a line on him?"

"Why?"

Grogan said: "I'll ask the questions. You just answer."

Hunter shrugged. "He's a client."

"When did you see him last?"

"Yesterday."

"What time yesterday?"

"Noon or so."

"On what business?"

Hunter's thin lips tightened. He knew there was trouble ahead. He said, "Personal business."

"Of what nature?"

"I can't tell you, Grogan. Confidential."

The big cop said, doggedly, "I got to know."

"Then ask Munoz."

"I can't."

"In that case . . ." Hunter opened his hands in a gesture of finality.

Grogan said, too casually, "He's dead."

Hunter made his face a blank.

Grogan said: "Murdered."

There was no reaction.

Grogan sighed, an ostentatious heave of his barrel-like chest. "Well, don't get all broken up about it."

"Lend me your shoulder. I'll cry."

Grogan bent forward to the attack again. "You saw him about noon yesterday?"

Hunter nodded.

"He hired you?"

Another nod.

"Gave you a retainer?"

"Yes."

"In cash?"

"Yes."

"Let's see the cash."

Hunter frowned, took the wallet from his pocket. He began to take the bills out of it. Grogan stopped him, saying, "Just give me the whole thing."

He took the hundred-dollar bills, spread them before him and began to check the numbers. After a moment, he nodded. He held up the bills: there were seven of them.

"These the ones he gave you?"

"Yes." He thought. And I've got five more in my pocket just like them and they give me the jitters.

Grogan frowned. "He gave you these at noon yesterday?"

"That's right."

"And you didn't see him again?"

"No," Hunter lied.

"It don't make sense."

"Why not?"

"The numbers don't run consecutively. There's two . . . then a couple missing . . . then five more."

"So what?"

"It oughta mean he saw you twice." He kept his eyes on Hunter's face. "You got nothing to add?"

"You got my story, Grogan. I'm stuck with it," Hunter said.

There was a moment of silence. Then: "We found him early this morning. In a car on East Sixty-second Street. Stabbed. Died somewhere else during the night. The car was driven there, left there."

He stopped, waited for Hunter to say something. The silence became heavier. Grogan sighed.

"We found your card in his pocket. Thought I'd mosey over and talk to you."

"Any leads?"

"Just you—if you wanna call this a lead."

"Thanks."

Again, the thick silence. Until Grogan said, "Sure you want to give me the lowdown about your business with him?"

Hunter hesitated. Every instinct directed him to tell Grogan all about it. Grogan was a good enough cop . . . doing his job . . . deserved all the help he could get.

But he said, "No. Not unless I have to."

There was disappointment in the big cop's face. His voice hardened. "You will."

Hunter shrugged. He watched the huge body lift itself ponderously out of the chair. The vast paw de-

47

posited the seven bills on the desk. Grogan walked out without a goodbye.

Hunter stared after him, fought off an impulse to run after him and tell him the whole truth.

But how could he? He didn't know what the truth was.

Besides, he could see the cop's face when he, Hunter, tried to tell him about *la calavera de plata*. The guy wouldn't believe a word of it.

6

HE WENT to the Garland after all—and one thing he soon learned. Phineas T. Shackleford entertaining a lovely lady was different from the black-clad character who'd slugged him earlier.

Suavely decked out in a tuxedo, he became a charming host—to judge from the frequency of Juanita Toy's laughter as she sat across a white tablecloth from him. And when, on occasion, Juanita's face did become serious and she leaned forward to ask quick questions, he just smiled them away with a wave of his hand. Obviously, Miss Toy learned nothing of her brother's whereabouts at dinner that evening.

And when, after the repast, Hunter leeched onto the Shackleford trail, he found himself in for another surprise. For the trail led to the Club Claw, "Cafe Society's Mecca."

More than that, Phineas was well known about the place. They took down the velvet rope and led Mr. Shackleford to a choice ringside table. Judging from the way the *maitre d'* hovered over him, he was a man who'd proved lavish in the past.

49

Hunter took up a position at the bar whence he could watch his quarry. He crooked his finger at the man across the mahogany.

The bartender leaned forward, eyes opened wide. They were knowing eyes: wise and tough. They'd seen everything—and had long ago lost all sympathy.

"I want to talk to you," Hunter said.

"Talk?" The tough eyes hardened.

"That's all—just talk."

Disgust crossed the bartender's face. "Goddammit," he brayed, "another one."

"Another what?"

"Every sonuvabitch and his brother gotta take his trouble to the man behind the stick." He shook his head. "All right, sonny boy," he asked disgustedly, "what's your beef? You got love trouble? Tell the barkeep. Money worries? Okay, I'll listen. Your dog—"

"Wait a minute, pal."

"Got worms?" the other tore on. "Tell *me*—I'm the expert. The market broke? Rest your weary head on my shoulder and weep—"

He stopped abruptly. Hunter had wrapped a five-dollar bill around his finger. The wise tough old eyes fixed on it. He smiled and his lovely red nose lit up like a lighthouse tower.

He said: "Excuse the running off at the mouth, pal."

"Forget it."

"It gets too much sometimes."

"Guess it does."

The bartender inched toward the finger that held the bill. The finger inched away to the same degree. The tough old eyes met Hunter's. "What's for the pound, pal?"

"Just some inside dirt."

"For the finif?" His eyes caressed the bill.

Hunter nodded.

"Ask it, pal. Ask it."

Hunter gestured at the table on the floor. "The old goat there at ringside—he make it this way often?"

"Phineas? Every night for the last week."

"Phineas?"

"Yeah. Phineas T. Shackleford."

"But—*Phineas* to you?"

With a name like that and a kisser like that—could you call him anything else?"

"I get your point," Hunter conceded.

At this juncture, the gentleman in question left his table, wended his way to a doorway behind the bandstand and disappeared through it.

"Where's he going?" Hunter asked.

"Miss Laine's dressing room, I guess. Or maybe—" He stopped.

"Maybe what?"

"Maybe Frank Moretti. Owns the joint," he explained.

"I've heard of him."

The bartender's fingers darted. The bill disappeared from its perch on Hunter's hand. The wise eyes measured him.

"Your time is up," the old man said. "Deposit five dollars for three more minutes, please."

Hunter made another five-dollar tube for his index finger. The wise old eyes brightened. "Fire away."

"Who's Miss Laine?"

"Our chantootsie."

"Phineas is her friend?"

A lewd wink veiled one eye. "A very good friend."

"Like *that?*"

"If Phineas has any *that* left, it's like that."

Hunter considered for a moment, then said, "He always comes alone?"

"Nope."

"You know who comes with him?"

"Nope."

"Ever see him with a Chinese girl?"

The bartender hesitated. He eyed the five-dollar bill. He said, "Well . . ."

Hunter said, "One or two more, that's all."

"Okay." He nodded. "A Chinese girl? Nope—not a *girl.*"

"What then?"

He looked at the bill pointedly. Hunter surrendered. The bartender smiled, stuck the bill into his pocket like a courtesan tucking the night's wage into her bosom.

"A young Chink feller," he said. "Was in last night. They was all together after the joint closed. Him and the Chink and Moretti and Miss Laine. A regular confab."

"What about?"

The wise old eyes flickered, went dead. "Mister, you just come to the end of the line. Phineas' business, I don't mind discussing. But Frank Moretti's—" He shivered.

Hunter shrugged. He knew he would get no more.

The bartender brightened. "Tell you what I'll do,

though. I'll buy you a drink."

"Good deal."

Hunter watched the amber liquor gurgle into the glass. "Thanks," he said. "Oh—and thank Mr. Moretti, too."

The bartender saluted, moved to the other end of the bar. After a moment, Hunter could hear him discoursing on the elements of the "very dry Martini."

Hunter nursed his drink until Shackleford reappeared at his ringside table. Immediately, a solicitous waiter appeared out of nowhere to minister to him.

The lights darkened. A dull floor show began. A chorus of tallish girls pranced across a dime-sized dance floor, only slightly out of step. A brightly lacquered master of ceremonies told some dirty jokes, then introduced a magician who performed a few tired tricks. The M.C. told a few more dirty jokes, then presented "the cute canary who's caroled her way into the hearts of New Yorkers—Miss Pat Laine."

Pat Laine came as close to being cute as any five-foot, ten-inch, one-hundred-seventy-pound girl could. Which is to say she missed it by several city blocks.

But she did have a charm of her own. Full bosomed, full hipped with strong full thighs, she was the embodiment of a pot-bellied businessman's secret sexual dream. She larded her voice with the professional tricks which, in the music business, simulate desire.

In spite of it all, she was good. Through the artificiality and the slick-as-plastic phoniness, there came a genuine yearning, a lost loneliness, that reached out and touched every man in her audience. As though there was a stratum of true emotion that *believed* the tired cliches she voiced. And when, for a finale, she did Gershwin's *Man I Love,* her voice had the hypnotic quality of a blue flame burning brightly in the smoke-filled dungeon.

She bowed off to tumultuous applause. As soon as she did, Shackleford called for his check. Judging by the benevolent smile of the waiter, he left too much tip.

After his quarry had gone, Hunter left the bar, skirted the struggling couples on the overcrowded dance floor and went through the door Shackleford had used earlier. He found himself fifteen feet away from a short flight of stairs. Between himself and the first step stood a moon-faced bulky young man in an over-draped tuxedo.

The moon-faced man smiled pleasantly. "Are you looking for someone?" he asked. His teeth were white and regular. His voice was soft. It was hard to explain why he looked so menacing. But he did.

Hunter pointed toward the stairs. "Miss Laine?"

The man nodded.

"I'd like to see her."

The round face registered disappointment. "Unfortunately, you can't."

Hunter reached into his pocket. The man's body tensed. Hunter's hand came out with a business card. The man relaxed.

Hunter handed him the card. It was simple. It said:

Peter Hunter

And chastely in the lower left hand corner:

Investigations

The guard held it gingerly between thumb and fore-finger. "Investigations!" Contempt larded his well-bred voice. His eyes searched Hunter from head to toe. "My," he simpered, "aren't we the big-shot?"

Hunter ignored the sarcasm. "Miss Laine would like to see me."

"No, she wouldn't."

"Suppose you make sure. Ask her."

The guard hesitated. The bulky body half turned. "Wait here," he snapped over his shoulder. He raced up the stairs, two at a time.

His footsteps sounded overhead. A door opened, slammed shut. There was silence for two minutes. Hunter lit a cigarette.

The door opened again. He heard the guard say, "Right, Mr. Moretti. Yes, sir, I'll dispose of him."

Hunter's jaw squared. The blue eyes froze. The expressive fingers curled in irritation.

The moon-faced guard still held the business card as he came down the stairs. He flipped the little square of cardboard into thin air. It described a little half-circle and fluttered down at Hunter's feet.

The guard's smile was pitying. "No dice, Mr. Investigations. Run along."

Hunter dragged deeply on his cigarette. He made no move to go.

The guard said, sharply, "You heard me, bum. Miss Laine isn't receiving."

"You didn't ask her, did you?"

"Mr. Moretti said no. When Mr. Moretti says Miss Laine isn't receiving, there's no point in asking Miss

Laine how she feels about it."

Hunter said, softly, "I'm going to see Miss Laine."

Jaw muscles bulged in the guard's round face. He moved toward Hunter, his hand reaching into his back pocket.

A cold flame flared in Hunter's ice-blue eyes. He watched the guard intently, but did not retreat.

The guard's hand came out with a blackjack. Just as it started its lethal swing, Hunter calmly flipped the lighted cigarette into the grimacing round face. The guard gasped, fell back. Without haste, Hunter took two steps forward, kicked the other in the shin.

The blackjack fell to the floor. Its owner doubled over. Hunter stiffened his hand, chopped it blade-fashion against the other's neck. The guard said, "Ugh," and pitched forward onto his face.

Hunter regarded the motionless figure with impersonal detachment, then stepped over it. He made his way upstairs.

This corridor was longer than the one below. He opened the first door he came to. A series of raucous feminine shouts greeted him. It was the chorus dressing-room. He withdrew his head without embarrassment.

He skipped the next and went to the far end. Black block letters identified it as:

CLAW ENTERPRISES, INC.
BUSINESS OFFICE

He turned away from it, went back to the one he had skipped. He heard humming inside. He turned the knob, went in.

"Hi," he said easily. Then, "Pardon *me*."

Pat Laine turned from the mirror. She said, "Hi," then, "What's the matter?"

He pointed to the bra she was holding. He said, "Restore the camouflage, please."

She looked down at her hand. "Narrow-minded, eh?" she said pleasantly.

"Mother warned me against them. Said to steer clear of such entanglements."

"If mother said so . . ." She shrugged, turned her back. He watched the encompassing process in the mirror. "I knew there was no truth to the rumor."

"Rumor?"

"About the falsies."

"If I ever need an affidavit—"

"Call on me."

She said, "Thanks, pal." She faced him. "That better?"

"Much." He grinned. "Mother'll be relieved, too."

"Good." She donned a blouse that deepened the blue of her eyes. "What's your grift, pal?"

He handed her the business card.

"Um—investigations."

He nodded.

"Does that make you a private eye?"

"That's the expression, I've been told."

She tapped the card against a very white tooth. An impish mischief danced in her eyes. "Frankly, Peter, I've always wanted to meet a *real* private eye."

His eyes warmed. "Your search is over."

She sighed. "I'm disappointed."

"So many are," he conceded sadly.

"You look like anybody else." The mischievous eyes inspected him. "Only nicer."

"Thanks—but don't get the wrong idea. I'm real nasty. I have gold teeth and brass knuckles."

"Thank goodness—I almost lost faith." Her lips twitched merrily. "That bulge near your armpit—is that a *gun*, Peter?"

"No ma'am—my wallet."

"Heavy, isn't it?"

"Makes me round-shouldered."

"Your feet are much too small."

"But they're flat. Very flat."

"Your ears have no lumps," she objected. "Your nose isn't pushed in. You have no knife scars—"

"Yes, I do. One."

"Let me see it."

He recoiled in horror. "Please—Miss Laine."

She shook her head. "You don't look the type."

He said, anxiously, "If you'll get a hammer—a good heavy one—you could fix my nose for me."

She laughed delightedly. In spite of her size, she managed to look like a little girl having a romp. "Thanks for indulging my little joke, Mr. Hunter. It was sweet of you."

"My pleasure, Miss Laine. Besides—the customer is always right."

"Customer? Me?"

He sighed. "I'm never that lucky."

"Thank you."

"You can help me, though."

"How?"

"I need information."

She frowned. "Sit down and tell me about it."

He shook his head. "I better stay near the door," he explained. "That character from downstairs'll be up after me any minute. I'll be safer here."

"The character from downstairs?"

"The one who guards the door."

"Oh. You mean Rocky."

"He said I couldn't see you. I had to clobber him."

Her eyebrows lifted. "You knocked him out?"

He nodded. Her lovely lips rounded into an "O." He basked in her admiration for a moment, then said, "I haven't much time, Miss Laine."

"Fire away, Peter. I may call you Peter, mayn't I?"

"I'd like it."

She laughed. "Good. I'm Pat." She extended her hand. He clasped it. The handshake was firm, the flesh soft and pleasantly warm.

Their eyes met. She said: "I *like* you, Peter."

"Mutual, Pat. But—" he disengaged himself gently "—I better get back to the door."

"I thought you private eyes—"

"We sure do. We're human. But business—"

"Okay. Shoot, Peter."

"Pat," his eyes were intent on her face, "do you know a guy named Shackleford?"

"Shackleford?" She frowned. "A little."

"Only a little?"

"A little more than a little, maybe. But why—?"

"I'm trying to find someone. A Chinese named Ramon Toy."

"Ramon . . . Toy?"

"His sister wants him. Before he gets himself in a jam."

"In a jam?"

"Say, are you a parrot or something?"

"Echo, they call me. I take the words right out of your mouth." She did not laugh. "Why are you telling me this?"

"She's afraid he'll murder someone."

The red lips parted. "Murder?"

"I thought you might know—"

"Me? Why me?"

"Because he pals around with Shackleford. Just like you."

A cloud veiled the blue eyes. They weren't candid any more.

"No, I've never seen this . . . Ramon."

"Never?"

"Never."

"Not even last night?"

It was a bull's-eye. Her mouth popped open. Strain pinched her nose.

He ground on relentlessly. "You talked with him only last night. You and Shackleford and your boss, Moretti. What about?"

She clamped her lips tight.

"A guy was murdered last night, Pat. Was that what you four spoke of at your conference?"

Another hit. Positive fear flared in the blue eyes.

"What's more, Shackleford—" He stopped.

Footsteps outside! Pacing down the corridor.

"Rocky." Hunter grinned mirthlessly. "Out for blood."

Her hand went to her mouth in fright. "He'll kill—"

He put a warning finger to his lips. She stopped.

The door burst open. Its arc shielded Hunter against the wall. The guard's voice was strident. "Where is the sonuva—"

Hunter stepped forward. Again, the blow which had felled the other earlier, the judo chop against the side of the neck. But not so hard this time. It didn't have to be. The shock of the first blow had not yet worn off.

He went down hard. He lay still. Too still.

Visibly concerned, Hunter bent and felt the pulse. He sighed his relief.

He rose. "Get this guy a doctor as soon as I leave."

She was frightened. She said: "Please go. *Please!*"

"Sure. You want to tell me anything first?"

She shook her head mutely.

He said harshly: "It's a rotten rap. Murder."

Her lips moved without sound. Speech seemed to have failed her.

"If the police start digging—"

"Please. Please go—before Moretti comes."

"Moretti!" He spat the name contemptuously.

"You don't know him," she cried. "He'll kill you. And it won't mean a thing to him. No more than swatting a fly."

He said: "Thanks for worrying." And left, swaggering.

But, once the door had shut behind him, the nonchalance disappeared.

Moretti!

MAKE WAY FOR MURDER

The very name was frightening. Because this was a guy with a gangland reputation. And he'd reached his pinnacle like any other gangster. Over dead bodies.

He shrugged his shoulders. His smile was rueful.

He thought: Oh, well—bring on the gangster, too.

7

HE LEFT the Club Claw immediately. Once out in the street, he ducked into a telephone booth and made a call.

"Garland Hotel," the voice at the other end answered.

"Miss Juanita Toy."

He listened to the ringing at the other end. Five times it sounded without attracting an answer. Hunter was about to hang up. Suddenly, breathlessly, the other end came to life.

"Hurry, hurry," a voice screamed, and it was hard to identify it as Juanita Toy's. "Come—"

A thud sounded. The voice stopped as abruptly as if someone had lifted the needle from a record. There was a light click: the phone being replaced in its cradle.

He sat in the phone booth, staring at its mute walls. What did he do now? Was she really a damsel in distress? Or was he being lured into a trap?

The walls had no answers.

He went back into the street, hailed a cab. It took ten minutes to push through traffic as far as the hotel. Peter Hunter sat in the back seat, scarcely moving . . .

His eyes gimleted into every corner of the hotel lobby

as he entered it. There was no one he recognized. The elevator whisked him to the ninth floor.

He stopped in the corridor, looked around. It was as if he were seeking some alternative course of action. But there just wasn't any.

With the enthusiasm of a man asking admission to the interior of Hell, he rang the bell to Juanita's suite. There was no answer.

He bent to look through the keyhole. He should have known better. It was a standard hotel lock, designed to foil Peeping Toms. The inner and outer keyholes were at different levels.

Now his hands tensed as they sensed something wrong. Something dreadfully wrong.

Instinctively, almost as if they were tired of doing nothing, his fingers darted into a side pocket. When they came out, they held a complete set of lock-picking tools —jimmy, tweezers, celluloid.

The lock presented no problems. Given a task to perform, the sensitive hands worked smoothly, efficiently. It took less than one minute to produce the click. He opened the door. The place was ablaze with light.

He burst through the small foyer, charged into the living room, then stopped short. Like one who'd butted into a stone wall.

There on the floor lay Juanita Toy—naked.

He thought: *She's dead!*

He stood there, almost out on his feet. The thump of pulsing blood pounded in his ears. Then he saw something and his face lit up. The rush of blood rose to a roar.

She was alive.

His keen eye had detected motion. She was breathing. Almost unnoticeable—but it was there.

He kneeled beside her. He took her hand, felt her pulse. He leaned over her body, touched his ear against the soft flesh in the hollow between her breasts, listened to her heart.

He turned away quickly, began to search the apartment. A quick glance showed the tiny kitchenette was empty. He went to the bedroom.

No one there, either. The closet door was closed. He opened it to make sure it was empty.

There was a faint sound within. A rustling noise—one he remembered and immediately identified. The soft whisper he'd heard when she was in his office.

He leaned inside to identify it. It was, even as he had predicted, an undergarment, a low-cut slip of scarlet taffeta. He took it in his hand, feeling the crinkle of the material, relishing the scent of the woman who had worn it. After a moment, he turned away.

There was a purse on the night table. He opened it, leafed through the contents: A bankbook in Juanita's name, showing a deposit of five thousand dollars made only a week ago; a receipt for an advance payment on a reservation for suite nine two seven; a check for a parcel at Pennsylvania Station; a key to a safe deposit box; the key to this apartment; a full assortment of cosmetics; and, most of all, that faint dry provocative perfume.

A soft moan sounded in the living room. He stuffed the contents back into the bag, returned to Juanita Toy.

She was stirring now. He bent to her and picked her up. In his arms, she weighed no more than a feather. He moved to the couch, put her down as gently as if he were handling a fragile priceless art treasure.

Again she moaned, stirred painfully. He went into the bedroom, returned with a blanket and covered her. He pulled up a chair beside the couch, massaged her hands.

Her face was very pale, the skin like transparent parchment with a faint delicate tracery of blue veins beneath it. Even as he watched, an eyelid fluttered . . . opened.

She looked at him uncomprehendingly. He smiled, said, "Hi."

A light of recognition glowed in the wonderful green eyes. She tried to answer his smile. The effort made her wince.

"You need a drink," he said. "Where is it?"

Weakly: "Kitchenette. The cupboard on the right."

He found brandy. He poured two stiff jolts, gulped one, brought the other to her.

She sat up, reached out a bare, beautifully formed arm to accept the glass. The movement upset the blanket. It fell, revealing her breasts.

With unflustered speed, she restored the covering. He met her eyes, found no embarrassment in them.

"A robe," she said, smiling softly. "In the bedroom closet."

She donned it while he pretended to go into the kitchen for another drink. When he got back, she was on her feet.

He said: "What happened?"

"How did you get in?" she countered.

"Jimmied the door."

"You met no one?"

"Only you." He pointed toward the rug. "Down there."

For the first time, he re-created the picture of her nakedness. The soft, smooth ivory of her skin . . . the flat pliant belly . . . the firm, softly rounded, subtly molded breasts . . .

He felt his face grow hot. She guessed his thoughts. A soft blush suffused her cheeks. But the green eyes sparkled.

He said: "Shall we change the subject?"

"It is so unpleasant?"

"I'm embarrassed."

"*You?*"

He grinned. "One of us ought to be. And, obviously, you're not."

Her face sobered. She sat down on the couch beside him. Her eyes were soft now. "I owe you a great debt, Mr. Hunter."

"Peter," he corrected.

"Peter." She made it sound like music. "Pete."

"You don't owe me a thing, Juanita."

"They wanted the letters." Her voice trembled. Her eyes widened. The terror eddied back into them.

"They?"

"Munoz's men."

"Munoz!" He thought: It's impossible. The guy's dead.

"They did not get them. They will never get them."

"But he's dead," Hunter said. "Munoz is dead."

"Dead?"

"Didn't you know?"

67

Her eyes met his unwaveringly. "No."

"I thought you did. I thought that's why you chose me to find Ramon. Because you knew I was working for Munoz."

She said nothing.

Hunter said: "He died last night. In my arms."

Still, she said nothing. Silence settled over the room—a heavy brooding palpable thing.

Finally, she moved. The slender graceful fingers came together and formed a pyramid. It was as if she was saying a prayer.

"Munoz was looking for something," he said.

"The letters."

"Something more. He died for it."

Her lips remained pressed together, silent.

He said, "Do you know what it was?"

Slowly, she turned to face him. The delicately formed lips parted slightly. She took a deep breath and the movement outlined her breasts against the thinness of the robe.

She said, "I do not know."

"He vowed they would never get it. Who are *they?*"

She shook her head. "I cannot help you."

"They finally killed him."

"Munoz was a determined man," she said. "A dangerous man."

"He risked his life."

"And lost." Her voice pronounced the judgment like a bell tolling a requiem.

"Stabbed to death. Murdered."

A vein began to throb in her temple. Her eyes were

68

shadowed now. Remote.

He said, harshly. "Your brother and Shackleford were discussing Munoz only last night."

"*Ramon!*"

"Also a gangster named Moretti."

The name evoked nothing. She was interested only in her brother. "Ramon spoke of Munoz? Last night?"

"It's significant, isn't it?"

The lovely face seemed to age. It developed a care-worn quality. She said, "How do you know all this?"

"You asked me to find out. I found out."

As though fearing to face the truth, she put her hands across her countenance. Her body began to sway gently in the slow, side to side rhythm of mourning.

He said, probingly, "You think your brother killed Munoz, don't you?"

It was as though he'd touched a vital point. Her hands jerked away from her face to disclose sharp lines of pain gouged in the flawless surface. Doubt and fear muddled the pure depths of her eyes.

"You've got to face up to it, Juanita."

"No."

"Why not?"

"Ramon wouldn't. He couldn't."

But the vein in her temple throbbed like a drum now. And her fists clenched so hard the knuckles showed white.

The telephone rang, a harsh jangle of dissonance. She started, inadvertently looked down to her wrist to see the time, then frowned because she wasn't wearing a watch.

"It's twelve-fifteen," Hunter said.

"At this hour—who could be calling?"

He shrugged. "Maybe those guys would like to come back."

She grimaced, picked up the instrument and said, "Hello." She listened for a moment, then turned to him. "A telegram," she explained. "Have you a pencil?"

He handed it to her. She hunched over, her back turned, obscuring the instrument as well as the message she was writing.

The only sound was the soft slur of the pencil on the paper. After a moment, she said, "Thank you," and hung up.

She was smiling. "Of all things," she said, and handed him the paper she had been writing on.

It said: *Arriving New York Friday morning Twentieth Century Limited. Look forward to seeing you. Boy will we have fun.*

"Who?" he asked.

"Henrietta! A girl who visited me in my native country."

"Oh."

She tried to walk back to the couch, wavered slightly and had to grasp an end table for support. When she felt steady again, she pressed her hands against her temples. A quick expression of pain shadowed her face.

He said, "I've been a brute, badgering you this way."

"You saved my life."

"I did, didn't I?" he asked jokingly.

"They had just come in. They held me and they demanded to know where the letters were. Then the telephone rang."

"Hunter to the rescue," he said dryly.

"They were surprised, I guess. That's why I was able to break away. I had only time to scream into the receiver before they tore me away. Then—" She touched her hand to her head, feeling the bruise beneath the hairline.

He said, "Well, I guess it's time . . ." He started toward the door, the words trailing off. Reluctant to leave, he turned, hand on the knob.

"Sure you'll be all right?"

"Quite sure, Peter."

"I could stay, y'know," he offered too casually. "Just in case."

"No. I'm sure it's safe now."

"Well, if you should need any help . . ."

"Thank you." Her gratitude was fervent.

"And if Ramon *is* in that jam . . ."

It was as though the thought of her brother's peril had dynamited the dam that held her emotions pent. "Oh, Peter," she blurted, "I'm frightened." Her face screwed up like a hurt little girl's.

She took a faltering step toward him. His arms opened and caught her. He said, "All right, Juanita—let it go. Let it all come out."

Come out it did. Under the stress of tears, her body shuddered like a cork on a wind-swept sea. He soothed her shoulder, waiting for the storm to subside.

Ultimately, the calm came. The trembling passed, the sobbing ceased.

71

A suspenseful hush settled over the room. He thought: She's over it now. Let it go.

But he held her. Something inside made him do so. He found himself tensed, holding his breath, waiting. A lump formed in his throat.

She raised her face. Began to say softly, shyly, "Pete, you've been so kind . . ."

His cold blue eyes met the warm green ones. Ravaged by tears, she looked like a little waif—lost, lonely and more lovely than ever.

They both knew what was going to happen. The choked-up feeling within him swelled until he felt he must burst under its pressure. He watched her eyes widen . . . saw the expectant parting of her lips. Blood began to pound in his head like a million drums.

He bent and kissed her.

Her lips were soft and warm and yielding—then suddenly hard against his.

Hot. Rough. Demanding.

His arm, around her shoulders, tightened, pulling the soft pliant body fiercely against his. The warmth of her body suffused him now . . . through the thinness of the robe she wore . . . through his own clothing.

His free hand undid the knot of her belt . . . slid beneath the encompassing fabric of the robe. A wild thrill of elation shot through him as his fingers made contact with her bare flesh. It was hot against his hand—yet soft, yielding, irresistible.

The hand beneath the robe went behind her, stroked her back in a rhythm he did not consciously will . . . a rhythm stronger and older than either of them . . . a

72

rhythm as old as time itself.

Her body swayed to that same immutable rhythm . . . pressed harder and harder against his body . . . until it seemed that her all-consuming desire was to melt and fuse those two bodies into one. He felt himself drunk with the cadence of their movement, with the drumlike beat of the pounding in his head.

But suddenly, she uttered an agonized little scream, tore herself away from him. Her eyes were tormented; her breast heaved. The robe was open. The lovely skin seemed to gleam like ivory in the softness of the light.

She spoke, and the words seemed to wrench themselves out of her unwilling lips. "Please, Pete—please, please go," she implored.

He took a step toward her. He said, "Juanita." His voice choked.

"Please, Pete. *Please!*"

He fled.

8

His brain bubbled like a boiling cauldron as he rode down in the elevator. As he crossed the lobby, he put his hand to his mouth reminiscently. It was as though he could still feel the Chinese girl's lips on his.

Out in the street, he found himself grateful for the refreshing coolness of the night air. It was late now, almost one o'clock. He turned west and walked to a cab parked at a hack stand near the corner.

The driver looked up inquiringly. Hunter opened the door and said, "Tail job?"

The cabbie turned in his seat. His was an all-knowing New York face. Nothing could surprise him any more. He had looked upon humanity in all its eccentricities.

He said, "At this hour, Mac?"

Hunter smiled. "Can you count?"

The cabbie shook his head sadly. "I ask the guy if he knows the time—the guy asks me can I count. This is an answer?"

Hunter handed him a bill. "Count that—and see how much time it buys me."

The driver looked at the bill. "A big ten."

"Humor me."

The cabbie shrugged. "You're payin'? I'm humorin'."

"Thanks."

The minutes dragged. Hunter sat tense, expectant. The cabbie concentrated on the entries at Jamaica.

Finally, he put his form sheet down and turned to his fare. "You said tail job, pal. What are we tailing? A ghost?"

"I asked you to humor me, didn't I?"

The hackie shook his head. He'd really caught a lulu this time.

Just then, Juanita Toy came through the hotel's revolving door. She carried nothing more than her pocketbook. The doorman blew a short piping blast on his high-pitched whistle.

As if out of nowhere, a cab materialized. Juanita stepped into it, speaking quick words to the driver.

Hunter leaned forward, spoke tensely. "There it is."

"The Yellow up ahead?"

"Stay with it."

"Like a leech, pal."

He threw the car into gear. The abruptness of his forward motion knocked Hunter against the back seat.

Then, just as abruptly, they jammed to a stop with an agonized squeal of brakes. Hunter lurched forward, almost bounced against the front seat.

He said, "Take it easy, buddy."

"You said stay with it, didn't you, pal?"

"Yes, but—"

"So I'm stayin' with it."

"I didn't mean to crawl all over it. You're almost up the guy's back."

"Well, how did I know the coward was gonna stop for the red light?"

Hunter leaned back. "Just keep it in sight."

"Okay, pal." The light ahead turned to green. The Yellow continued eastward. Fifty feet behind, Hunter's cab followed at a sedate pace.

At Second Avenue, their quarry turned south. "We still tailin', pal?" the hackie asked over his shoulder.

"Still tailing."

"That dix is wearing awful thin, pal."

"There's more where it came from."

They were approaching the lower Thirties now. The Yellow turned east again. Hunter's driver said, "He's headin' for the tunnel."

"Just another block, then."

"He's goin' into Queens." The cabbie made it sound as if this was the height of insanity.

Reluctantly, Hunter said, "Okay, drop him." He gave the driver his home address.

He knew now where Juanita Toy was going. He frowned. The further he went with this thing, the worse it got.

He was still frowning the following morning when, as he was about to breakfast on bitter black coffee and aspirin, his doorbell rang. He answered it to find the huge bulk of Inspector Kevin Grogan hulking outside his threshold. With him there was another equally large gentleman in a quiet, well-tailored blue suit whom Grogan introduced as simply a Mr. Matthews.

Hunter stood in the doorway, eyed his visitors curiously. Grogan cleared his throat to say, "Mind if we come in?"

Hunter's grin was mischievous. "Got a warrant?"

"I can get one if I have to."

"Then I'd better submit quietly." He stepped aside.

While the two men waited in the living room, Hunter excused himself long enough to go back to the kitchenette and pour the coffee down his throat, washing down the aspirin in the process.

His visitors looked up when he returned. Hunter said, "Well, what can I do for you, gentlemen?" Although his lips wore an easy smile, the guarded expression never left the cold blue eyes. His hands had tensed themselves into a defensive alert.

"I got more questions about Munoz," Grogan said.

Hunter's lips continued to smile, but the blue eyes were even colder. They turned to inspect the man called Matthews. The latter said nothing. He merely sat impassively, his gaze never leaving Hunter's face.

Grogan turned to Matthews as though asking permission to begin. The other granted it with a slight nod. The huge detective's head swiveled back to face Hunter, eased itself forward ponderously.

"I been following some leads," he said.

"So?"

"More and more, you fit into the picture."

Hunter waited.

"I looked into them hundred-dollar bills. Munoz spent

77

a couple during the afternoon the day he saw you. I got them back. They turn out to be the two that are missing from that sequence of yours."

"So?"

"So this: you must have seen him later than twelve noon yesterday in order to get those last five you had."

Hunter said, easily, "What are you trying to do, Grogan—railroad me?"

"Huh?"

"Making a force-fit on me!"

Grogan clenched huge fists. "Why, you punk—"

"Because it doesn't follow, Grogan. You know it. You're just faking a case."

Grimly, the huge cop shook his head. "You're cute. Hiding behind a confidential relationship. Thumbing your nose at the law." A garish grin seamed his face. "If it was up to me, I'd run you in. I'd wipe the sneer off your face."

The big head swiveled toward Matthews. Grogan's face pleaded with the other one. The man in the blue suit shook his head expressionlessly.

Like a man accepting a distasteful order, Grogan sighed. Woodenly, he said, "We got more."

"Better than the story of the bills, I hope."

"We'll see. We place you in the neighborhood where the body was found earlier the same night."

"Interesting."

"Is it? The cop on the beat identified your mug. Said he saw you hanging around. Even lit a cigarette for you."

"That's a crime?"

78

"The doorman remembers you."

"What else?"

"An elevator boy took you upstairs into a certain building."

"For God's sake, Grogan—come to the point."

"The point is this: There's a man living in that building who—"

"All right, Grogan." The words came from the man called Matthews. They were low, but commanding. Grogan broke off without finishing the sentence.

Grogan picked himself up angrily. "What the hell's the sense of my going on with this phoney waltz?" he demanded harshly. He was talking to Matthews. The man in the blue suit said nothing. "If it was up to me," Grogan had a full head of steam now and he rumbled on like a runaway tank, "I'd throw this grinning P.I. into the can and work him over. I'd hit him with the rubber hose until he unbuttoned his pretty little lip."

The man in the blue suit shook his head.

Grogan turned away. "I'm gonna get the hell out of here. Do any damn thing *you* please. But remember"—he stopped to wave a menacing finger at Hunter—"if I dig up any more on you, punk, into the can you go. No matter what anyone else says."

The man in the blue suit finally spoke. "All right, Inspector, I think you'd better go."

Grogan slammed his hat on his head angrily and slammed the door hard on his way out.

The man in the blue suit turned to Hunter. His square face had an impassive quality, one that bespoke a man who kept his thoughts to himself. Even his eyes seemed to curtain themselves against revealing anything.

Matthews said, "I'm here to talk about this Munoz case, Mr. Hunter." His voice was pleasant, but he uttered his words with a finality that brooked no argument.

Hunter shrugged his shoulders noncommittally. "Okay," he said, "let's talk."

"I trust you will be franker with me than you have been with Inspector Grogan."

Hunter said nothing.

"As you have realized by now, this Munoz affair is more than the ordinary sordid New York murder."

"It's been kept out of the papers somehow. That has to mean something."

"It must stay out of the papers, Mr. Hunter. That is why we haven't allowed Inspector Grogan to take you into custody."

"He doesn't have enough to—"

Matthews stopped him by raising his hand. "Let me finish, Mr. Hunter."

Hunter gestured acquiescence with open palms.

"Thank you." The man in the blue suit leaned forward. His impassive face hardened into deadly earnest. "I can tell you this—and no more. Munoz was an important official of a Latin-American country. He was here on a delicate mission." The curtained eyes narrowed. "Do you know what it was?"

"He was looking for something."

"Exactly."

"He hired me to negotiate for it."

"Ah." The meaning of the sigh was hard to decipher. "Did he tell you what it was?"

"Not exactly."

"Let's be precise, Mr. Hunter." The voice was sharp as a dagger. "Do you know or don't you?"

Hunter said: "He didn't confide in me."

Matthews leaned back, relieved. "Good."

"However," Hunter said off-handedly, "I gather that it might have been something he called *la calavera de plata*. A silver skull, or something." Though his manner had been casual, his eyes focused on the face of his visitor to read the effect of the words.

There wasn't any reaction. After a moment, Matthews permitted himself a small smile. A smile at once pitying and sardonic.

"Don't fish with me, Mr. Hunter," he said. "I'm here to get information—not to give it."

"And you've gotten all you're going to get," Hunter flared.

Matthews shook his head. "No, Mr. Hunter—you're going to cooperate with me completely."

"Why should I?"

The man in the blue suit leaned forward again. His manner carried a deadly earnestness. "Because, Mr. Hunter, the security of your country is involved. You are concerned with a matter that affects a nation only one hundred air miles from the Panama Canal. The balance of political power is delicate there. Munoz was an important factor in the situation. The reaction to his death is something no one can foretell. But remember—this is an affair of incalculable gravity."

Hunter stared at the other, undecided. Finally, he asked, "What can I do?"

"Give me information."

"What information?"

"Who killed Munoz?"

"I don't know."

"Any guesses?"

Hunter hesitated. "Not yet."

The man in the blue suit noted the hesitation, apparently decided not to question it. He said, "Do you know what Munoz was after?"

"No."

"Or who he was trying to get it from?"

"He thought Shackleford had it."

"He doesn't?"

Hunter opened the eloquent hands. "That's all I know."

"You have no idea who has it?"

"Some people seem to have the idea," Hunter said slowly, "that I have it."

"Why?"

"I don't know."

"And do you have it?"

"Not yet."

Matthews rationed himself another small smile. "You don't even know what it is—but still you hope to get it?"

Hunter said, sharply: "Don't worry. I'll get it."

Their eyes locked. After a moment, the small smile disappeared from the big man's face. "I shouldn't be at all surprised if you did, Mr. Hunter," he announced thoughtfully.

"Thanks."

"And when you do get it, Mr. Hunter, you will turn it over to me."

Hunter said nothing. The smile on his face was too cryptic to be read.

Matthews said doggedly, "I am sure you will."

Hunter said, abruptly: "If there are any more questions you want to ask . . ."

The man in the blue suit shook his head. "Any further questions," he said regretfully, "would be apt to provide you with more information than they do me."

Hunter said, grinning wickedly, "I could use a little light."

Matthews hesitated. "If it were up to me, Mr. Hunter, I would let you into my confidence." He sighed. "Unfortunately, I have my orders."

"Too bad."

Matthews shook his head. He rose slowly and went to the door. He said: "Let me impress it on you, Mr. Hunter. This matter is deadly serious. The security of your country is at stake."

The big man's veiled eyes uncurtained long enough to reveal a blazing intensity, then went guarded again. In a moment, he was gone.

Peter Hunter stared at the closed door fully five minutes after his visitor's departure. Finally he shook his head ruefully.

He spoke aloud, and his mouth twisted as if the words he uttered had a bitter taste.

"*International* complications," he said. "The only thing that was missing."

9

He had the feeling they were closing in on him. Grogan was hot on his trail. He'd found the cop on the beat, traced Hunter to Shackleford's apartment the night Munoz was killed. He'd keep moseying around, Grogan would, and pretty soon he'd fine someone who'd seen Munoz arrive at Hunter's apartment on his way to dying.

Grogan was that kind of cop, he knew. Thorough, patient and dogged. When he started something, he finished it.

Hunter rose and went to the telephone. After he'd reached his connection, he interrupted the correct secretarial response at the other end to say, brusquely, "This is Peter Hunter—I want Mr. Dwyer."

An amused male voice took the other end. "Yeah, Pete, what kind of trouble you in now?"

"Not yet—but you're going to start earning that retainer I pay you."

The voice at the other end continued to smile. "With you, Pete, I'm always earning it."

"Grogan will be locking me up in a day or two."

"Grogan?" Tommy Dwyer's voice took on new respect.

"What will the charge be?"

"Murder, probably."

"That all? And what do I do?"

"Get me out."

"How?"

"How? Any way you can—that's how. That's your problem. You're my lawyer, aren't you?"

Dwyer pretended to sigh. "That I am, my boy. And although it's not always easy, it's often interesting. By the way, how will I know you've been incarcerated?"

"That's why I'm calling. I think Grogan will probably pick me up quietly and haul me off to one of those precinct dungeons where he can work me over without anyone knowing about it. I want you to check with me every day to make sure I'm still at large."

"Can do. I'll have my secretary—"

Hunter exploded. "The hell with your secretary. I'm paying you!"

Dwyer's sigh was longer this time. "Okay, Peter—just as you say."

Although it was late afternoon, Pat Laine was still in pajamas when Hunter rang her bell. He found flattering, to say the least, the mixture of surprise and pleasure with which she greeted his appearance. At her hearty invitation, he followed her into a cheerful dinette where she proceeded to dispense robust roast beef sandwiches and excellent coffee.

Sitting at a gaily yellow formica-topped table, his mouth full, he asked, "Hey, what gives? All this food—

you trying to eat yourself out of a job?"

She tossed her taffy curls disdainfully. "Singers work hard. They have to eat." Her hands outlined her attractively ample figure. "I'm a big girl, remember?"

"Yeah, but what about fashion?"

She grinned. "I'd rather eat."

"Right out of a job?"

"I'll do a Kate Smith."

"You could," he conceded. "You got enough voice for it."

"For that, you can have more coffee."

"Thanks." He extended his cup. "It's good."

"Funny . . ."

"What's funny?"

"Today, it's nothing but nice things. Last night . . ."

He said, "Oh . . ."

She poured the coffee, then lifted her eyes to meet his. "By the way, what *does* bring you here? The food?"

"Not exactly."

"Certainly not the girl?"

He said, earnestly, "Pretty soon, maybe, but—right now—" His face molded itself into a comic-melodrama leer. He put his finger to his lips. "Shh—I'm sleuthing."

"Here?"

"Where else could I get fed this good?" His face sobered. "Seriously, though, I'm in a jam. I have to find out who killed Munoz."

"You have to find out? Why you?"

"Because the police are sure I killed him. And I don't hanker to spend the rest of my life in the can for a murder I didn't commit. And besides, people seem to think that I have whatever it was he was after."

"But why come here?"

"Because you know what I don't know."

"And what's that?"

"Why he was killed."

She recoiled from him in sudden distaste. "What a nasty thing to say."

"So I'm a nasty guy," he said simply.

She said: "I'm afraid I can't help you?"

"Can't? Or won't?"

"Can't," she insisted.

"Look," he said. "Munoz was cut down because he wanted something very badly. Something that you and Moretti and Shackleford and Ramon Toy also wanted. And God knows how many other people. Someone was afraid Munoz would get it—knocked him off."

"It's as simple as that, is it?"

He didn't answer her sarcasm. Instead, he asked: "What is this thing—*la calavera de plata*—that everybody's so hot about?"

Her eyes widened in fear. "What do you know—?"

"Because if that's what you guys are after—I mean that *calavera* thing, whatever it is—you've gone and killed the wrong guy. Munoz didn't have it, couldn't get it."

She leaned forward. "And you have it?"

"Not exactly."

"But you can get it?"

His head moved in a gesture that could have been interpreted as a nod. His face came closer to hers until there were only six inches separating them. "You tell

Moretti I'll be in my office in about two hours. I'll listen to his proposition."

Her lips parted. His eyes held hers. He came nearer and nearer until, for an instant, their lips met. She put her hand to her mouth after he had moved away. There was wonder in her eyes.

He answered her unspoken question. "Anyone who can sing Gershwin the way you do . . ." He let the words trail away.

Pleasure wreathed her face. She said, "Why, Peter, that's the nicest—"

He broke in abruptly. "Don't forget to give Moretti my message."

Perhaps it wasn't the wisest thing to do, he reflected two hours later as he made his way up to his office, but what other way was there? Knowing, even as he asked the question, that there wasn't any answer.

Knowing, too, that there was no other choice . . . that the way to solve some human equations, unlike those of mathematics, was to wade in swinging, knock the unknown factors around until they were battered into a shape that made sense.

There was only one reservation: Would a guy like Frankie Moretti hold still for that kind of treatment?

The answer came sooner than he expected, soon enough to deepen his respect for the gangster. It came as soon as he switched on the lights in the office.

There, sitting behind the desk was the man called Rocky, the one he'd knocked out last night. Only this time the bulky, moon-faced thug was leaning back and pointing a gun at him.

The man smiled softly, showing the perfect ring of very white teeth in his pleasant fact. But there was that in his eyes which made Hunter realize the punishment of the night before had not been forgotten.

"Mr. Hunter, I presume? Investigations?" It was still the same soft, well-modulated voice—but tonight it carried a deadly undertone.

"Stop making like a ham villain," Hunter snapped. "What's your pitch?"

"Mr. Moretti sent me, Mr. Hunter. He said to bring you back with me."

"Is that all?"

"Not quite, sir." The smile was mirthless. "I'm hoping you'll decide you don't want to go."

Hunter said bitingly: "With a gun in your hand, you become a big man, don't you?"

"Don't taunt me, Mr. Hunter." The voice became almost inaudible now, the menace of it even more deadly. "I have a stiff sore neck, Mr. Hunter. I know who gave it to me. I'd love to pay the man back for it."

Hunter measured him, muscles tensed, wondering whether he could jump the man, take the gun away.

Rocky looked into his face, read his intention. The thug's eyes lighted up. "Please," he begged. *"Please* try it."

"You're too anxious."

"You don't know how anxious I am."

"I'll do it later," he promised.

"I can hardly wait."

"Moretti wants me now?" Hunter asked.

"Not tomorrow."

"Let's go then."

Rocky followed him carefully. When they got into the elevator, his captor stood, gun in pocket, a little behind him, leaning against his prisoner so that Hunter could feel the steel pushing against his body.

Out in the street, the man with the gun said, "Turn to the left. The gray Cadillac up the block."

There was a little man sitting behind the wheel. He looked up as they approached. "Got him, hah?" he asked. "Any trouble?" He had a face shaped like a carrot, with skin colored to match.

Rocky said: "Unfortunately, no trouble." And to his captive: "In the front seat, Mr. Hunter."

The little man behind the wheel covered Hunter as he slid into the car. Rocky got into the back seat, directly behind Hunter. He put a handkerchief over the gun.

He said: "Lean back, Mr. Hunter."

Hunter obeyed. Now he could feel the gun barrel boring into his shoulders.

"If you make the slightest move, Mr. Hunter—I would just love it."

Hunter said, "You want me to get a stiff neck?"

Rocky touched the back of his own neck with his free hand. "A very stiff neck, Mr. Hunter. Cold and stiff."

"Ham actor," Hunter muttered. But he didn't move the rest of the trip.

The car pulled up to the back entrance of the Club Claw, the one which Hunter had used in making his escape last night. When it stopped, Hunter focused his attention on the driver.

Again, the little man covered him as he got out. Again, he felt Rocky's gun take over the job. But Hunter's eyes were still fixed on the little driver, hoping passionately that he would not accompany them inside.

It was like a prayer answered when he heard the motor start, the car drive away. Because that left him alone with Rocky. And, although the moon-faced tough had the artillery, it was not Hunter's intention to let him hold it much longer.

Rocky said: "The door is unlocked, Mr. Hunter. Open it."

Hunter thought: It's not hard to take a gun away from a man, even though he has it in your back.

"Thank you, Mr. Hunter—this way."

But you have to be quick. You have to be sure. You have to know you can do it.

Because this is a game in which you can't make even one mistake, one false move . . .

"Now, up those stairs, Mr. Hunter."

He thought: All right, Hunter—what are you waiting for?

He took a quick step to his left. His right arm went back, clamped Rocky's gun hand against Hunter's body. Hunter's left hand swooped down to grab the gun hand at the wrist and twist. Now, the right arm drove back, the right elbow smashed into Rocky's face.

It was lightning fast: each movement of the sequence flowed into the next one like the rippling motion of a rattlesnake striking.

He heard Rocky grunt. He increased the pressure on the gun hand. The weapon dropped out, he caught it before it hit the floor, turned with it in his hand to face the onslaught.

His face splattered with gore, Rocky charged. Hunter met the attack with a left-hand blow to the pit of the stomach. Rocky doubled over. Hunter brought his knee up hard. It crashed against the other's forehead.

Rocky's knees buckled. Hunter rapped the gun barrel sharply against the side of his assailant's head. The tough pitched forward onto his face.

Hunter caught the unconscious form before it hit the floor. He lifted the bulky body over his shoulder with surprising effortlessness, carried it as if it were no more than a side of beef.

He slipped Rocky's gun into his pocket and, bearing Rocky's dead weight easily, he trudged quietly up the stairs.

At the head of the stairs, he stopped to listen. There was silence. The scuffle had been so short, so quiet, that it had attracted no attention.

He moved on. This time he didn't stop at any of the intermediate doors in the corridor. This time he went directly to the one marked:

CLAW ENTERPRISES, INC.
BUSINESS OFFICE

He stopped to take a deep breath, then squared his shoulders. He twisted the knob. The door was unlocked. He pushed it open, walked in.

There was an artificial redhead sitting at a typewriter desk. Her red mouth popped open at the sight of him. Her jaw went slack. She blanched to the black roots of her hair.

"Where's Moretti?" he demanded harshly.

10

THE REDHEADED girl's frightened lips moved, but no sound issued from her mouth. Scowling, he started toward her. Her terrified eyes picked out a door for him. He barged through it.

He found himself standing in a vast room which seemed only slightly less vast than the Grand Canyon. At its far end there stood a magnificent desk at least eight feet wide, its top a solid slab of bleached mahogany some two inches thick.

From off to a side came a bored voice. "What the hell do you want, doll?" it asked.

He turned to face it. It emanated from a man who lay flat on his stomach on a stone table. There was a towel draped across him from his knees to the small of his back. He had lifted his head and was looking at Hunter. He had a hard handsome face with strikingly deep brown eyes and it admitted to perhaps forty years.

He wasn't alone. A masseur was half suspended in the act of leaning over him, rubbing him down. Sitting beside the stone table was a silver-haired, silver-eyed girl working on his fingernails.

Hunter began to move forward. The man on the table watched the approach narrowly. If he felt fear, his face didn't show it.

"You Moretti?" Hunter demanded.

The man on the table didn't answer. His face remained expressionless. But the manicurist, her silver eyes wide, nodded inadvertently.

Hunter strode closer, eased the unconscious burden that was Rocky gently down. It went to the floor without a sound.

"This," Hunter announced harshly, "belongs to you."

The brown eyes of the man on the table inspected the formless heap on the floor. They lifted to inspect the man who had delivered it. They said nothing.

Finally, he spoke. "What's the pitch, doll?"

"That's what I came to find out from you."

Again, the inspection from the brown eyes. Carefully, this time: an assay, a weighing-up process. When it was finished, the man on the table had obviously come to a decision.

He rose to implement it. The silver blonde in the chair released the hand she had been working on. The towel fell away, leaving him naked.

It was a beautifully proportioned body he was exhibiting . . . broad at the shoulders and through the chest, yet narrow-hipped and flat-stomached. He paced his way to the magnificent desk at the other end of the room, his eyes fixed on the ceiling. Finally, he turned from his deep thought.

"I'm going to deal with you, doll." He turned to the masseur and the manicurist. "I'm going to meet him half way," he said.

They nodded as if they understood him. The silver-haired girl evinced no embarrassment at his nudity. She might just as well have been looking at a tree.

He said, "All right, everybody beat it and leave me with the new doll."

They started to leave. "Chris," Moretti called. The masseur turned back.

"Take that with you."

That was Rocky.

The masseur grunted, managed to get the dead weight to his shoulder.

"Chris."

The masseur waited.

"Dump it somewhere."

The masseur nodded, left.

Moretti flipped a switch that lighted a long strip of fluorescent tubing in the ceiling. The illumination was soft, flattering. It gave his deeply tanned skin a healthy glow. He went behind the massive mahogany desk and sat down.

Narrowed, the brown eyes inspected Hunter again, repeated the assaying process. "So you're the private eye, doll."

Hunter let the remark pass.

"I wanted to talk to you."

He didn't seem to find anything in that worth picking up, either.

Moretti leaned forward, rested a bare arm on the desk, pointed a steady finger at his visitor. "Doll," he said, "find yourself another corner to peddle your papers."

Hunter ignored that comment, too. He fixed his gaze on the ridges in Moretti's flat washboard stomach.

Moretti stood up, smiling broadly. He came out from behind the desk. "Doll," he said, "I like you. I sit here, running off at the mouth, you ignore me. When I talk business, you'll listen. Until then, you clam." He extended his hand to be shaken. "Doll, you got sense."

Hunter looked down at the proferred hand. Contemptuously, he knocked it away. The icy blue eyes blazed with a cold fury. Jaw thrust forward pugnaciously, he leaned toward Moretti.

"I don't like you, Moretti. I don't like a fraud who tries to four-flush me by faking that he's unloading a guy in front of me. I don't like a phoney who wastes my time by saying nothing after he's sent for me. And most of all, I don't like a guy who poses in the nude for me like a goddam piece of tail."

Moretti's face stiffened. A deadly menace shadowed the brown eyes. Muscles tensed under his tanned skin. Hunter braced himself against an attack.

As the menacing brown eyes measured him, Peter Hunter had the feeling that he was just the next breath away from death. But then, just as swiftly as it had hardened, Moretti's face relaxed.

"Doll," he said, "I like you. I said I like you before, and this time I really mean it." Almost affectionately, he clapped Hunter on the shoulder. "Don't go away, doll."

He stepped past Hunter and pressed a button. A panel slid back. He stepped through the newly formed doorway. The panel slid shut again.

Hunter sat down to wait. His nerves jumped as he

heard a soft hiss. After a moment, he identified it as the noise of the shower Moretti was evidently taking. Five minutes later, his host was back, fully dressed, and looking antiseptically clean.

Moretti returned to his position behind the desk, briskly this time. He opened a drawer and took out a checkbook. "Let's talk business, doll," he snapped.

"Good."

"You got it?"

Hunter pretended ignorance. "Got what?"

"What I want."

Hunter's lips smiled. His eyes remained cold. "Why d'you think I'm here?"

"Okay, so you got it. What's the price?"

"Make an offer."

"Five grand."

"Peanuts."

"Remember this, doll." Moretti turned the menacing brown eyes on his visitor and the feel of his glance was like the breath of the Angel of Death. "I don't have to offer anything."

"No?"

"No. I could make you decide you want to give it to me."

"I doubt it."

"Don't doubt it, doll. Believe it."

"All right, so you could. But you'd rather not get it that way."

"Right."

Hunter said, with slow smiling impudence: "Moretti, I think you're getting soft."

"Maybe I am, doll." A look of embarrassment came onto his face. "Maybe I am."

"Then you'd better raise the ante. Because you're talking chicken feed."

"How do I know you got it?"

"Because I say so."

"When can I get it?"

"As soon as the dough's right."

"How much do you want, doll?"

"I told you once: make me an offer."

"Ten grand?"

"Still peanuts."

Moretti frowned. "How much do you think the damned thing is worth altogether?" He began to tick off the cost factors on his neatly manicured fingers. "Let's say twenty-five grand for the platinum in it — and that's a good offer."

"And the rest?"

"The stones we got to fence. They'll have to be cut up. Can't use 'em the way they are. Say I'm lucky—another hundred seventy-five grand. Say two hundred grand altogether."

"And you have four shares."

"Four?"

"Pat Laine," Hunter began.

"Scratch her. She's out."

"Three, then. You, Shackleford and Ramon."

"Ramon? Oh, the Chink. No, he's Shackleford's headache."

"So there's only two."

Moretti's grin was deadly. "Not two—one."

"Not even Shackleford?"

"If I get the damn thing from you, doll, why the hell should I feed the old man?"

"So you get the whole two hundred?"

A bland smile. "You catch on quick, doll."

Hunter's smile was just as bland. "Maybe I ought to take the whole thing myself."

"Don't try it, doll."

"Why not?

" 'Cause *I* want it. Want it real bad."

"That's a reason?"

"You know a better one, doll?"

"Maybe not." Hunter rose. "But you'll have to talk louder, then."

"My last word." Moretti leaned toward him. "Twenty-five grand."

Hunter turned away. "I'll think about it."

A vise-like hand clamped onto his shoulder, twisted him back. "Don't think too long, doll."

The face of the other came closer to his. The brown eyes burned into his brain. Hunter felt like a man being measured for a coffin.

Moretti said, musingly: "I'm beginning to get a funny feeling about this whole kick, doll. I'm beginning not to like it."

"Funny? Funny how?"

Moretti's strong finger came up under Hunter's chin, lifted it firmly. "Don't think I'm braggin', doll—but how many guys you think I knocked off in my time?"

"I give up. Tell me."

"Maybe thirty-five. Maybe forty."

"So?"

"Remember—I ain't braggin'. It was always business. And one more don't make any difference."

He fell silent, his thoughts obviously turned inward. Hunter waited, uneasily.

"But sometimes, doll, I think of a helluva joke. You know what I think of?" The striking brown eyes were fixed on Hunter's face again.

"Spill it, Moretti. Let me laugh, too."

"Yeah, joke. Sometimes I tell myself: 'Moretti,' I say to myself, 'some day you gonna let one guy get away. Just one that you shoulda bumped. And that's the guy who'll pull the whole house down.'" The burning eyes bored into Hunter's. "See what I mean?"

"Not exactly."

"Forty guys knocked off. And 'cause I let the next one go, it's all wasted."

Hunter said: "I'm beginning to get you."

"One last thing—the most important." The fire in the brown eyes blazed into a conflagration. "I almost get the feeling, doll, that you're the guy. So . . . don't try me, doll. Don't try me."

101

11

WITH ABOUT as much relish as a cow chewing her cud, Peter Hunter ate a very fine dinner that night. His mind kept ranging back to the sequence of events that had led him to Frankie Moretti—and would lead him even further. But, now that he was no longer in direct action, his nerves began to get jumpy.

Uneasily, he drained the last of his coffee. It had always been like this for him. When he was in motion . . . doing things . . . throwing his weight around . . . his confidence in himself was boundless. It seemed to rise spontaneously out of the roots of action.

But, when the period of inaction came . . . and there was nothing to do but wait . . . then stealthy doubt assailed him.

He thought, petulantly: You and your muscles. Sticking your neck way out. Trying to push people around till they fall into the line you want.

What the hell was so smart, he asked himself, about telling Moretti that you had a *calavera de plata*—or whatever the damn thing is that the gangster wants? Chances are, the bum'll be after it with a hot rod if you don't turn it over to him by tomorrow.

Tomorrow . . .

Tomorrow, if his plans worked out right, they'd all be after him. That is, everyone but the one who actually had the damned skull. He tried to visualize the ensuing events but the effort at quiet concentration was too much for his nerves.

He rose jumpily, threw a bill down on the table and went back to work like a man pursued.

It was Ramon Toy who answered Hunter's push at Phineas Shackleford's doorbell. The young Chinese manifested no surprise at the identity of the unexpected visitor. The flat face remained completely phlegmatic, the dark eyes inscrutable.

They stared at each other warily for a moment. Then Hunter said, "I want to see Shackleford."

The young Chinese turned without a word. He disappeared into the rear of the apartment. In a moment, the long thin eel-like body of Phineas T. Shackleford made its appearance. The older man's sharp spade-like face wore a questioning smile.

"My dear young fellow," Shackleford bubbled, "this is indeed a gratifying surprise. Why, I had no idea—"

"Spare me the effusion," Hunter cut in. "I'm here to talk business."

Phineas's manner warmed. "Here to talk business, eh? Splendid." His voice had the stridency of a crow's. "We'll have a cozy profitable chat." He motioned Hunter to a seat opposite him. "And what shall we talk about?"

Hunter hesitated, drew a deep breath. He had to take

103

the plunge now. It was all or nothing.

"*La calavera de plata*," he snapped. "The silver skull."

"Well said, Mr. Hunter. Directly to the point." The smile broadened. It seemed incredible that that long lugubrious countenance could summon up so much cordiality. "Very well, then—we'll talk about the skull, by all means. Make yourself comfortable. And tell me what you will drink."

"Scotch. With water."

"Scotch, it will be. *And* with water. By all means." He clapped his hands and, like a genie, Ramon materialized out of nowhere. Shackleford spoke rapid words to the young Chinese in a singsong language. Ramon left, returned with a bottle.

Hunter looked at the label. It was Ambassador. He said: "Never mind the water."

"Good, Mr. Hunter. It is, indeed, a nectar too heavenly to suffer dilution."

Hunter grunted, said nothing. The thin man turned to Ramon, uttered sharp sounds in the strange language. Ramon shrugged and left the room again. Hunter watched him with suspicious eyes.

"Do not alarm yourself, Mr. Hunter. I merely asked him to bring us ice."

Ramon returned with a silver bowl full of cubes. He put it on a table, stood waiting for further orders.

Hunter said, "That's swell. Now ask him to leave us alone."

"You do not like Ramon?"

Hunter looked at the stolid face of the young Chinese. "He makes me nervous," he said.

"Really now, Mr. Hunter, Ramon wouldn't—"

"Get rid of him."

Shackleford bowed, addressed the young Chinese in the foreign tongue. Evidently, Ramon resented the request. His black eyes flashed as he spat words back at Shackleford. The older man repeated himself at greater length in a more conciliatory tone, adding a spate of detail.

Ramon seemed to calm down as he listened, began to nod. Although his face did not change, Hunter got the impression that something had pleased him. He went to a closet and got his hat. On his way out, he turned at the door.

"Good night, Mr. Hunter," he said in perfect English. "I trust we shall meet again."

The door closed behind him. Hunter shook his head. Somehow, he'd gotten the impression that English was not among the young Chinese's accomplishments. And now to hear him express himself in purest Oxford accents.

The discomfiture in his face caused Phineas Shackleford to emit a chuckle.

A nervous nasty chuckle . . .

The uneasiness it evoked in him caused Hunter to remember the first time he had heard that sound. It had been when Munoz had asked him to call the eel-like man and open negotiations.

It had, at the time, seemed such an easy way to pick up two hundred bucks.

"An astonishing boy, Ramon," Phineas was saying. He poured the liquor generously, lifted his glass for a toast. "Just the two of us now, Mr. Hunter. For a quiet *tete a tete*. Shall we commence talking?"

Hunter lifted his own glass in reply, sipped at the drink. It fairly melted its way into his guts. He reacted with an appreciative sigh.

Shackleford leaned forward. "And now, directly—about the skull."

"Suits me."

"Very well, Mr. Hunter. I have one question. A direct question. An unequivocal inquiry. To wit: How much do you want for it?"

Hunter leaned back indolently. He said: "I've already had one offer."

The long face frowned. "Indeed?"

"Twenty-five thousand dollars."

"Twenty-five thousand dollars." Miraculously, the frown was replaced by an indulgent smile. The smile deepened into delighted laughter. Still, he sounded like a crow.

He repeated the words. "Twenty-five thousand dollars, Mr. Hunter? For so priceless a property? A mere bagatelle. Why, that would be to defraud you, my good man. Pure larceny. And petty larceny, at that."

"You'll go higher?"

"Much, much higher, believe me."

"All right, then—let's stop beating around the bush. What's your offer?"

"First, let me establish one thing, Mr. Hunter." Shackleford leaned forward intently. There was a faint dew of perspiration on his long upper lip. A tense fire glittered in his dark eyes. "You have it, sir? You *actually* have it?"

Hunter laughed teasingly. "Come now—you can answer that. You were the first to know, weren't you?"

Shackleford chuckled in relief. "So I was, wasn't I?" He shook his bony head wonderingly. "Although where you hid it—"

Hunter grinned. "I have my secrets, y'know."

"I actually saw it come to you, Mr. Hunter. With my own eyes. And Munoz—he knew about it too, didn't he? No wonder you had to kill him."

Hunter stiffened. "Kill Munoz?"

Shackleford waggled a bony finger. "Very well, admit nothing. Quite right—a prudent policy, I do confess. Even the walls have ears. Exactly."

Hunter said: "Let's get back to the subject for the evening."

"A sound point, sir—to stick to the point, if I may venture the pun. Very well, sir—here is what I propose." He straightened up, stretched forth a long lank arm dramatically. "A full partnership. Equal shares. Nothing less."

"Very generous."

"You don't find it so?"

"For you to share what's mine with me?"

Shackleford inclined his head. "An argument in your behalf, granted. But—and mark this well—without me you would merely sell the object for its metals, its precious stones. Is that not so?"

"What else could it possibly be good for?"

"What else could it possibly be good for, he asks?" The old man laughed aloud. "An excellent sense of humor. Now, sir—let me put a question to you: How much would a man pay to become the absolute ruler of a nation? A small nation, it is true. But nevertheless, a nation . . . an *entire* nation. How much in cash?"

Hunter lifted a palm from the arm of the chair it rested on to indicate an incalculable amount. He thought: This is more like it. Now we're learning things. If only the old man keeps running off at the mouth.

Shackleford's strident voice knifed into his musings. "Think of it, Mr. Hunter. We have in our possession—"

"*We?*" Hunter snapped. "*Our?*"

The old man brushed the objection away with a disdainful wave. "Yes—because I am certain you will cast your lot with mine. To repeat: we have in our possession a power as strong as an army. Nay, far stronger. We have the one sure guarantee of complete and total political dominion."

"We have?"

"We have. *But,*" and here the long lugubrious face composed itself into a cunning grin. "I am the only one who can conduct the negotiations successfully. *I* am the only one completely conversant with the full ramifications of the situation. Hence, Mr. Hunter—my valid claim to full equality in the proceeds."

"You do have something," Hunter admitted.

"We both have something," Phineas amplified. "It is an ideal partnership. A perfect marriage."

"And how much would you say our ideal marriage was worth in cold cash?"

"A down-to-earth question. A mundane question that bespeaks a hard practical mind. And I like that. I am not one to sneer at practicalities. But let me reply to your question with another."

"Go ahead."

"Very well then, I answer you thusly: Suppose I were to go to De Sola and say: 'I have it, sir. Without it, you are no longer the leader. Without it, you are—poof—gone.' How much would he pay to get it? Remember—he has millions in his treasury. Literally millions."

"It does sound big."

"Big! It is, in the argot of our film capital—stupendous, colossal."

"Okay." Hunter drained the last of his drink. "Now tell me this: How do we handle Moretti?"

"Moretti?"

"Your partner. At any rate, your erstwhile partner. The guy who offered me the twenty-five grand. How do we get him off our backs?"

The look on Shackleford's face was pure smugness, the cat who had eaten the canary. "That, Mr. Hunter, is the beauty of our position. The eternal beauty of simplicity. We are engaged in a self-liquidating project."

"How so?"

"Simply this, sir: De Sola has depth, De Sola has resources. We simply say: 'It is one of the conditions of the transaction that certain individuals be deprived of the ability to render us any harm!'"

"Meaning Moretti."

"Exactly. And De Sola—in order to possess himself of what *we* have—will do the necessary—er—cleaning up."

"As simple as that."

Delight at his own cleverness caused Shackleford's elongated face to shine. He leaned forward to tap Hun-

ter on the knee, a gesture he endowed with great significance. "It was I who sought Mr. Moretti out, Mr. Hunter. I played the fool for Miss Laine until she brought me
to him. I played the weakling for that gentleman because
I felt I needed his strength to acquire what I sought. But
always, I knew that when the—how shall I say?—*show-
down* came, I had available to me the necessary means to
control him."

"Clever. Very clever."

Phineas beamed. "You will find that I am not deficient
in gray matter, sir."

Hunter said, casually, "And how do you propose to
handle *me?*"

The older man raised horrified hands. His face became
pure as a prayer. He said, earnestly, "Believe me, Mr.
Hunter—I have entertained no such thought . . . no such
intention."

"I don't believe you."

"But sir—"

Hunter got up to go. "I'll leave you with this: I'll
think it over."

"Excellent. I assure you that when you have compared
my offer with Mr. Moretti's—"

"I'll let you know."

"Good."

"Tomorrow, maybe."

"In the affirmative, I'm certain."

"If I do go along with you—"

"And you will. I'm certain of it. Why, you would be
blind—"

"We'll handle it this way. You'll get in touch with

110

your parties, get an offer from them. After I have my share of the cash *in hand—*"

"A simple matter. Believe me, utterly simple."

"*And* your Mr. De Sola has taken care of Moretti—"

"Which he will do without the slightest tremor, I assure you."

"Then I'll turn the damn thing over to you."

Shackleford's face registered boundless admiration. "Remarkable, Mr. Hunter. Remarkable. A foolproof plan of campaign. It protects me from having the object taken away by force. And, of course, it places you in an impregnable position. I congratulate you, sir."

"The more you tell me how safe I am," Hunter said dryly, "the more I look for a hole to crawl into."

"By all means, sir, maintain your caution," Shackleford said. "And most of all, with Miss Toy."

"Miss Toy!"

The thin man waved a warning finger. "A dangerous woman, Mr. Hunter. Exceedingly dangerous."

"Not soft and cuddly—like you, for instance?"

"Oh, I'm aware I'm no match for her in pulchritude."

"Modest of you to admit it."

"Nor can I fire a gun as expertly as she, either."

"A gun?"

"A crack shot, Mr. Hunter. A deadly eye and an unwavering hand."

"A regular Annie Oakley."

"I beg your pardon."

"Skip it," Hunter advised wearily. "It's a local joke." He turned away from the older man. "I'll let you know. Maybe tomorrow."

111

Shackleford seized his hand before he could go. "A wonderful association," he crowed. "A *profitable* partnership."

The skinny man chuckled as he led Hunter to the door. That was the last sound Hunter carried away with him. Shackleford's chuckle.

The nervous nasty chuckle . . .

12

IT WAS PAST ONE in the morning now. He was on his way home. The streets were empty. He was tired.

He had a feeling of having been defeated. In vain, he told himself he had outwitted Shackleford. He had given nothing, yet learned a great deal. Still, he could not shake the sense of having lost.

He looked up at the windows of his apartment five stories into the sky. They were dark. He strained his eyes trying to detect movement. There wasn't any.

He thought: Who's waiting for you up there, Hunter? Ramon—with the knife? Or maybe Moretti's Rocky?

Rocky! Was it only eight hours ago that he'd over-powered the thug and delivered him to his master? It seemed more like eight years.

He thought: Well, you've gone and shaken things up good, haven't you? They all figure you for the damn whatever-it-is, now.

No, not all. Not Juanita Toy. He'd tried to call her and invite her to put in her bid. But there'd been no answer from her room.

He wondered where the beautiful Chinese was now.

His eyes strayed up to his windows again. Maybe she's up there, he thought. Gun in hand. Crack shot—waiting for him . . .

He made his way up. He was talking to himself softly by the time he reached the hallway.

Let's keep it quiet, he was saying. No sense telegraphing your approach.

But no, if there was anyone there, they knew already. They'd seen him coming down in the street.

He relaxed, tried to make his progress normally noisy. At the door, he paused.

He forced himself to be casual. He scratched the key against the lockplate, then inserted it into the keyhole. He turned the key. The lock swung back.

He took a deep breath. Now what?

He opened the door.

His eyes, accustomed to the light of the hallway, found the blackness opaque. Without hesitation, Hunter removed his hat. Still standing on the threshold, he thrust it forward at the level of his head. His body started to move in behind the hat. But, at the last moment, it stopped.

Abruptly, something hard swished through the air. Brutally, it dashed the hat from his hand to the floor. His fingers stung from the glancing blow.

He thought: Move, goddammit—move. Before they zero in on you.

The quick hands reacted. One of them found the light switch, snapped it on. The other grasped the hand of his attacker.

He stumbled inside, fighting desperately to maintain

114

his precarious hold on the wrist he'd grabbed. He lifted his head, came face to face with his assailant. The tigerish yellow eyes of Ramon Toy blazed into his.

He read those eyes and his heart sank. The message there, clear and brilliant, was jubilation, triumph.

There was good reason for Ramon to feel that way. For his grip on Ramon's wrist was slipping. Hunter realized only too well that he couldn't maintain it too much longer.

And, in the hand that Hunter could not control, the Chinese held a gun.

You asked for it, he thought savagely. *You stirred them up.*

But now he could no longer afford the luxury of self-condemnation. Ramon's implacable face was close to his. And Ramon's incredibly strong wrists forced the gun they struggled for higher and higher. Up, up it went— to the point where the Chinese could level it at the man who grappled with him so desperately.

Feverishly, Hunter cast about for a means of upsetting the other's domination. If he could only reach him with a butt . . . a kick . . .

His hold began to slip. His balance, an uncertain thing at the beginning of the struggle, teetered precariously, caused him to lose leverage.

Hunter felt his feet begin to slide out from under him. In a second, the deadly weapon would be pointed at his chest. Ramon's face was alight with victory.

He felt himself slipping . . . slipping. There was a sudden exertion of what seemed to be superhuman force by the young Chinese . . . accompanied by a triumphant grunt.

Hunter knew then that it was all over. He was lost. Irrevocably and irretrievably lost.

He stiffened against the final blow. He saw Ramon's eyes widen. A clap of thunder sounded in his ears. A hot blast singed his cheek. Ramon's body shuddered, went slack.

Hunter felt no pain. He fell backward. His head hit the floor. A bolt of lightning seemed to strike the top of his skull. He knew then that he was dying.

He thought: *So this is how it feels when you get it.*

Then the blackness roared over him and he accepted it gratefully.

So this is what it's like, he thought, when you've crossed to the other side. This darkness . . . this sense of overwhelming weight holding you down . . .

And the sounds . . . the faint distant weeping—was this part of death, too?

He wanted to try to open his eyes, but he didn't dare. He feared he would be unable to.

He lay there, motionless, consciously examining death.

But the will to be alive . . . to be free . . . was too strong to be suppressed.

Open your eyes, damn you!

Fearfully, his lids fluttered open, then slammed down shut against the pain of the light stabbing into them.

For a moment, he was stupefied. Then came the tremendous surge of joy.

Alive!

His head was splitting. His stomach felt as if it were caught in a vise.

But he was alive.

He gathered his strength. Sobbing, he pushed up with all his might. The overwhelming weight that pinned him to the floor suddenly rolled off.

He sighed. A soft wordless prayer of thanks surged up from the depths of his heart.

He was free.

He opened his eyes again, this time kept them open. They saw walls, windows, that meant something to him.

Yes, this was his home ... his room ... but what had happened?

Why wasn't he dead?

Again, his ears registered the sound he had previously identified as weeping. This time he turned toward it. Amazement widened his eyes until it seemed they must pop out of his head.

Juanita!

Juanita Toy ... sitting there in his chair ... crying.

Slowly, he sat up ... got to his feet. Then he saw the dark shape on the floor.

Ramon.

And yet, not Ramon. For the Chinese had been vibrant with menace, deadly. But this—this was just a hulk of flesh ... a slack unwilled blob of matter ... a face as empty as a full moon on a winter's night ... the top of the head a bloody compote of bone and hair and oozing gray matter.

It was Ramon who was dead.

Ramon dead and himself alive? How had it come about

—this unexpected inversion? What had caused the reversal?

Now, the whimpering in the corner stopped. Attracted by the sudden silence, he turned to it. Juanita Toy had raised her head. Her mouth was open, her eyes wide, staring incredulously.

"Pete!"

It was a joyful scream. In an instant she had sprung from the chair and was upon him, her arms around him, her face covering his, her lips hard upon his mouth, her warm wet tears salt upon his tongue.

They clung to each other for an eternally long moment. Then doubt came into his eyes. Gently, he disengaged himself. Slowly, he knelt beside the cold lifeless lump on the floor. His fingers went toward the gun, now resting a few scant inches from the hand of the motionless corpse.

He didn't touch it. Instead, his hand recoiled from it. He looked up into the lovely tear-filled eyes that now regarded him wonderingly.

He said, softly, "He wasn't your brother after all, was he?"

Mutely, she shook her head. Fear clouded those shining eyes.

"Why, Juanita? Why?"

Words rushed headlong to her lips. Her lovely voice took on the intensity of pleading. "How else, Peter? How else could I get you to help me?"

"Help?" He seized upon the word. "Help for what? What kind of help?"

118

"Against Munoz. Against Shackleford. Against all of them."

"But why? Why did you need help? What are you trying to do?"

"Pete . . . Pete . . ." Her voice broke. Her hand cupped itself into a beseeching gesture. "Please . . . don't ask questions."

He seized the imploring hand, pulled her down toward him roughly. Stumbling, she almost pitched against the dead body. She recoiled violently. He held her firmly in the kneeling position, her face opposite his, his eyes boring into hers.

"You've got to tell me," he insisted. "I've got a right to know."

The sea-green eyes met his frozen blue ones with regretful defiance. "I cannot tell you. It is forbidden."

In spite of his anger, he found himself thrilling to her beauty. He hardened himself against it.

He asked, with soft intensity, "Is it *la calavera de plata?* The silver skull?"

Her jaw dropped in amazement. "You know about it?"

He nodded. "I know."

And thought wryly: I know—but I wish I knew more about what it is I know.

He said: "I know a little, that is."

The wonderful green eyes lighted up radiantly. An ecstatic smile wreathed her face. "How wonderful!" Her tone was exultant. "If you know a little, then I may tell you the rest. And when I have told you, we shall work together as partners." She rose from the kneeling position, pulling him with her.

119

Her arms flew around his neck. "You will help me free my people. You and I together will accomplish the task for which I live."

He suffered her embrace without responding to it. He drew away, looked into her eyes. "You'll have to tell me all about it first."

"Pete, Pete—only too gladly. Now that I may do so in good conscience . . . without being accused of breaking a confidence. Instead, I am acquiring an ally."

Still, his eyes searched her. As though he feared a trick, as though he suspected her of a concealed weapon almost.

"Right now," she said. "This very minute, I will tell you all I know." She took his hand, tried to lead him toward the sofa.

He held back. His eyes went to the corpse on the floor, moved to the gun beside the dead hand, stopped there. He shook his head, but his eyes remained inscrutable.

Finally, he turned to her. "It's a long story?"

"Very long. But," she waved her hand gaily, "we have time—"

He stopped her with his hand. "No, we don't."

"But why not?"

"The police of this city have strange ideas, Juanita. When a man dies violently," he paused and again his eyes went back to the corpse in the center of the floor, "they want to be informed. And quickly."

"But must it be now, Pete? Now?"

He smiled wryly. "A killing—"

"Killing!"

Still once more, his eyes sought out the body of

Ramon. It was as though he was hypnotized by it. "You could hardly say he expired of natural causes," he explained finally.

"But it was self-defense, Pete—"

"That's what I hope to convince the police."

"And I will corroborate the story."

"You?"

"But of course, Pete—didn't I see the whole thing?"

"You saw it? But how—"

"The door was open. I saw it happen."

His mind went back to the struggle with Ramon. He retraced his actions, one by one. The opening of the door . . . the trick with the hat . . . the realization that he needed light because the Chinese's eyes were already accustomed to the darkness.

One hand, he remembered, had snapped the light switch; the other hand had grappled with Ramon's gun hand. Therefore, the door must have remained open, as she said.

Once enmeshed in the scene, he was powerless to resist following it to its conclusion. Sweat broke out on his brow as he recalled the animal triumph in Ramon's eyes . . . felt again the desperate horror as the Chinese inexorably turned the weapon against him . . .

But then, something had happened. What?

"I thought I was a goner," he said.

"It was Providence," she said simply. "I thought that surely I would die. For you were falling and Ramon was about to kill you. But, as you went down, your foot struck his. He twisted away—" and here the horror tinged her eyes "—and fell. The gun turned in upon him and went off." Her voice died away to a sigh. "I thought you had both died . . ."

He said nothing. For a moment, they were both aware of the loudness of the silence.

But he said, suddenly, "All right, baby—on your way."

"On my way, Pete?"

"I'm calling the police."

"And you expect me to go now? But you need me to corroborate—"

"No, Juanita, I don't need you. It's an open-and-shut case of self-defense. And I don't want you to be badgered by the police."

"Badgered—poof!" She managed to look like a rebellious urchin. "How can I go now? You are in trouble."

He took her hand, led her toward the door. "You're going," he insisted. "And right now."

For a moment, she seemed about to defy him. But he was too confident to be doubted. Suddenly, the radiant smile lighted up her face. She leaned forward, kissed him lightly on the cheek.

"It shall be as you desire, Pete." And even as she smiled, she was gone.

For a long, long minute, he stared at the blankness of the door that had closed behind her, his eyes masked, his face frankly puzzled, the eloquent hands alert, the restless fingers moving, moving, ever moving . . . As though they probed the atmosphere of this room for the answer to his bewilderment.

He shook his head doubtingly. His right hand doubled into a fist, smashed against his left palm. He went to the phone and dialed a number.

"Homicide?" he said to the voice at the other end. "I want Inspector Grogan."

13

THIRTY MINUTES later, Peter Hunter's apartment was a maelstrom of police activity . . . a seemingly unorganized chaos of individual specialists, each going his own separate way without regard to any of the others.

Flashbulbs exploded from all corners of the room as the photographers registered all the angles . . . little puffs of gray dust marked the path of the fingerprint gatherers . . . the long ribbon of metallic tape snaked its way through the apartment as ballistics took its measurements . . . above the bloodstains on the rug, almost like a Moslem at prayer, squatted the chemist.

And, over the myriad activities, scarcely seeming to move, yet unmistakably everywhere, brooded the vast figure of Inspector Kevin Grogan. Grimly unsmiling, he had asked a few quick questions of Peter Hunter upon arrival, and thereafter had avoided him. The big bulk moved from expert to expert absorbing spot impressions; the huge head leaned down to examine what they pointed out to him, the asphalt gray eyes seeing everything, revealing nothing.

The chemist rose and approached Grogan. "There's an

old stain in the rug, inspector. Looks like blood, too. Want me to take it?"

"Everything," Grogan snapped. "Everything you can get."

The fingerprint man made his report. "At least five different sets," he announced. Grogan nodded, said nothing.

The coroner entered, bustling. Grogan took his arm before he could get to the body, pulled him aside, spoke to him in short inaudible sentences. The coroner's eyebrows lifted. Without answering, he bent over the lifeless form, examined the grisly head with professional interest.

After a moment, he called Grogan to his side. As the big detective bent over the corpse, the coroner pointed, with a pudgy finger, to the side of the shattered head, made soft comments. Grogan nodded quickly. His huge head swiveled so that, for a moment, his baleful glance fell on the chief suspect. Whatever it was the coroner showed him, it seemed to bode no good for Peter Hunter.

The cameraman locked up his equipment, came to Grogan before leaving. "Got everything, Inspector."

"Good. Print 'em right away."

The man's face grimaced pain. He made a big production of consulting his watch. "Tonight?"

"Tonight," Grogan barked. "I want 'em ready when I get back."

The cameraman sighed. "Okay, tonight it is." He hurried off.

The plainclothesman on duty at the door came in to say that the newspapermen outside were yammering for entry. Grogan's reply was characteristically curt. "Hell with 'em." The guard shook his head, went back to the door.

The chemist left . . . the morgue wagon came and picked up the victim . . . the fingerprint men gathered up their specimens . . . and, as ballistics was reporting they had taken all the required measurements, a commotion developed at the door. The guard came back.

"Guy at the door," he reported. "Says he's this guy's lawyer. Wants in."

Grogan hesitated.

Hunter's grin was impudent. "I got my rights, Grogan," he said.

Grogan's sigh was a cavernous rumble in the barrel-like chest. "Bring 'im in."

"The reporters—" the guard began hopefully.

"Out."

The guard shrugged, went back to his post. After a moment, the blond cherubic figure of Tommy Dwyer, Hunter's attorney, bounced into the room. He waved a soft white hand at Grogan. "I don't know what the charge is, inspector, but he's probably guilty as hell," Dwyer said.

"Took you long enough to get here," Hunter growled.

"My dear Pete, in the middle of the night—"

"And zip up your fly. If you're going to be my lawyer, you'll have to be presentable."

Dwyer remedied the oversight in his toilette without embarrassment. He looked around the room. "Looks like you're in a real jam," he said, with apparent satisfaction.

"You like that, don't you?"

"But of course, Pete. Why, if you stay out of trouble, I'll have to work for a living—" He broke off abruptly, turned on Grogan. "How long do you plan to keep my client on these trumped-up charges, inspector?"

Unperturbed, Grogan waved a huge paw. "Give me a minute, counsellor."

Dwyer smiled. "Sure. By the way, Grogan—what *are* the trumped-up charges?"

Grogan sighed, looked up from the white-handled automatic he'd been examining. "We'll come to that in good time, counsellor," he said patiently. "All in good time."

Dwyer beamed cherubically. "Remember, Grogan, this is America. Habeas corpus, writ of mandamus and all that stuff, y'know." He turned to Hunter. "How'm I doing, Pete?" The grin was almost fatuous.

"Swell. You'll be on the Super-Chief to Hollywood any day now."

"While you rot in jail without my expert services, eh, Pete?"

Hunter shrugged. He knew that behind the comic air a keen mind was functioning. Anyone who regarded Tommy Dwyer as a fool was apt to get a rude comeuppance in court.

Grogan put the gun down on an end table, came back to Hunter on the sofa. "All right, boy," he rasped, "tell me all about it."

Dwyer said, quickly. "You don't have to—"

Hunter stopped the lawyer with an impatient hand. "I told you once, Grogan."

"Tell me again."

Hunter sighed acquiescence. "I came home tonight,

found him ransacking the place. We fought for his gun. I fell down, cracked my head. When I came to, he was dead."

"A clear-cut case of self-defense, inspector," Dwyer said quickly.

"That's all, Hunter?"

"That's all, Grogan."

"It's a thin story—"

"Give me time: I'll fatten it up for you."

Grogan leaned back, squared the vast shoulders. There was an enigmatic look in his eyes. "Maybe you'll have to, son. Anyway, I wouldn't want to be in your shoes." He rose ponderously. "Okay, let's all take a ride downtown."

"Wait a minute, Grogan," Dwyer interjected sharply, "what's the charge?"

"Let it go, Tommy," Hunter said. "I want to go. And right away."

Dwyer faced him incredulously. "You nuts, boy?"

"Maybe I am."

Dwyer snorted. "Maybe?"

"And I want a paraffin test as soon as I get there," Hunter said to Grogan.

"You'll get whatever tests we want to give you," the big detective snapped.

Hunter whirled to his lawyer. "Get an expert, Tommy."

Dwyer's mouth popped open. "At this hour of the night?"

"The hell with the hour. Get one." His eyes snapped to Grogan. "This bastard's so anxious to hang me that—"

Dwyer sighed. "Okay. I'll have one later."

"Not later. Now. Do it now. Get one on the phone."

Dwyer shook his head in resignation, started toward the instrument.

Grogan stared fixedly at Hunter. "What the hell's on your mind, boy?"

"I don't want to be framed."

"Framed! Why, you young punk, I've never framed—"

"There's always a first time."

"But the paraffin—what's this fuss with the paraffin?"

"You heard me. I don't want—"

The big detective cut him short with a wave of a huge paw. "Okay, boy, you'll get your test." He turned to Dwyer. "Never mind, counsellor."

Dwyer nodded at Hunter. "Well, Pete?"

Hunter nodded. "Inspector Grogan's word is good enough for me, Tommy."

"Trusting soul," Dwyer remarked sadly.

Hunter looked from his lawyer to the huge detective. "All right, gentlemen," he said, "let's go down to the Bastille." The movement of his quick hand was almost a flirting gesture. "After *you,* inspector."

Two hours later, the three of them sat gray-faced in the office of the district attorney: Grogan, glowering and implacable; Peter Hunter, silent now; and Tommy Dwyer, incredibly dapper at four-thirty in the morning, pounding on the table and shouting his argument at Buford Gardner, the assistant district attorney who had taken charge of the case.

Gardner, a thin sallow-faced man who affected a pince nez, listened to the lawyer patiently. Ultimately, when he had a chance to speak, he began to go over the facts in a patient, nasal tone.

"I admire your zeal, counsellor," he said to Dwyer, and he smiled sourly, "but let's summarize again. First, the murder occurred—"

"Murder?" Dwyer snapped. "What murder?"

"Very well, counsellor," the district attorney conceded, "homicide."

"That's better."

"It nevertheless occurred in your client's apartment. The coroner finds death from gunshot wound. Your client admits to firing the gun—"

"I do not." Hunter bit off the words.

Gardner's eyebrows lifted. "But you testified to a struggle—"

"That's all—just a struggle. I never said I fired the gun." .

"A struggle during which this weapon went off, is that it?"

Hunter didn't answer.

"My client never fired that weapon," Dwyer insisted. "He's being held merely because a vindictive inspector, pursuing a grudge—"

Grogan grunted. "We'll see soon enough."

"Nonsense." Dwyer went back to pounding on the table. "Either you charge my client here and now—"

Grogan said: "I ain't so sure the damn thing went off while they were fighting."

Hunter's eyebrows lifted. A look of respect for the big detective came into his face.

Dwyer asked, with elaborate sarcasm, "And what put

that thought into your mind, Grogan?"

"No powder burns on the wound."

"Interesting."

"Maybe he wasn't killed in the struggle. Maybe there never was a struggle. Maybe—"

He broke off as the door opened. A clerk entered with a sheaf of papers in his hand. He said, "The results of the dermal nitrate test, Mr. Gardner. You said you wanted them right away."

"Ah!" The district attorney's sigh was adenoidal. His thin sallow face took on an air of expectation. He took the papers, leafed through them.

Hunter leaned forward intently. Grogan's huge bulk stiffened. Tommy Dwyer said, "No matter what the tests show, Gardner, I demand—"

Gardner said, very suddenly: "It's negative."

Grogan exploded. "The hell you say."

In reply, the sallow-faced district attorney handed him the papers. Grogan's eyes ranged through the typewritten report incredulously. When he had finished he looked up angrily.

"It's a goddam trick of some kind," he bellowed. "I should have known when he demanded it—"

"That's enough of that, Grogan," Dwyer snapped. He turned to Gardner. "I think you've detained my client long enough." He turned to Hunter. "All right, Pete— let's go." They rose.

Grogan barred their passage toward the door with his huge body. Unbelievingly, he spoke to the district attorney. "You gonna let him walk out of here?"

Gardner's thin eyebrows climbed up his sallow forehead. "What else would you suggest, inspector?"

"Hold him."

"Indeed? On what charge?"

"Murder."

"The victim died of a gunshot wound, inspector. Remember?" The district attorney's voice became irritatingly sarcastic. "The coroner's report is quite clear on that point. And the paraffin report you hold in your hand indicates that Mr. Hunter has not fired a gun tonight. Suppose *you* tell me how a man who has not fired a gun can commit murder by gunshot wound, inspector."

Dwyer said, goadingly, "It must have been suicide, inspector."

"Nuts."

"The gun went off in the struggle, Grogan. While the victim held it. A clear-cut case of self-defense."

Grogan ignored the dapper lawyer. He stood facing them, his head lowered. The breath came whistling through his nostrils. He looked like a bull at bay.

As though he still couldn't accept the district attorney's verdict, he said to Gardner, "You mean you gonna let him go?"

"Unless you give me a charge I can hold him on."

"How about," Dwyer offered, "offending the delicate sensibilities of an inspector of police?"

Grogan flushed at the irony. But he would not be swayed. He set his square jaw doggedly. "Murder," he repeated.

The district attorney smiled disagreeably. "Without firing a gun?"

"I don't care what the report says." Grogan pounded a

hamlike fist on the table. His voice had a note of desperation. *"You gotta hold him!"*

In answer, the district attorney swiveled around in his chair. Grogan found himself looking at an unresponsive expanse of well-tanned leather.

There was a moment of tenseness. Then Dwyer said, "Okay, Pete, let's go."

He stepped around the big detective. When Hunter started to follow, Grogan moved as though to detain him. Their eyes met for a long second. Then Grogan's shoulders sagged in admission of defeat.

Hunter's face softened as he looked at the big cop. For a moment, it seemed as if he were about to say something to Grogan. Then, he seemed to think better of it. He joined his lawyer. The two men left unmolested.

Out in the street, the sky was a leaden gray, heavy with the threat of rain. They walked together in silence for half a block.

Then Dwyer said, "Oh, brother—is that Grogan after you!" He looked sidewise at his companion, but there was no response forthcoming.

"He was sure he had you all wrapped up—like a cat in a bag."

Still, Hunter said nothing. He walked along with his eyes fixed on the pavement.

"You'd better keep your eyes open, though," the lawyer continued irrepressibly. "He'll have the knives out for you from now on—"

"Tommy." Hunter's voice was dull as he interrupted.

He turned to face his companion. The lawyer was shocked at the deep lines etched into the face of his client.

"Yes, Pete?"

"Do me a favor?"

"Anything."

"Please shut up and go away."

Dwyer's mouth popped open. He started to speak, then snapped it shut angrily. Without a word, he stalked off. He didn't turn around until he had traversed almost the remainder of the block.

Peter Hunter was still standing where the attorney had left him . . . a weary sagging figure. His tired head lolled forward. His shoulders drooped. He seemed almost in a state of collapse.

For a moment, the dapper lawyer was tempted to go back to him. But even as Dwyer turned, Hunter, apparently conscious of the other's scrutiny, made a great effort and pulled himself erect. At a slow lagging pace, Hunter moved off in the opposite direction.

Dwyer watched him for a moment, found him a pitiable figure. Then he remembered Hunter's dismissal of him and shrugged, began to walk away.

He had gone perhaps twenty paces when a sudden thought caused him to stop, amazed.

For the first time in their many years of association, Tommy Dwyer found himself feeling sorry for Peter Hunter!

14

IT WAS five o'clock now. Peter Hunter's feet literally dragged as he walked down the street toward his house again. His face was gray now, grayer even than the leaden sky of dawn above. His cold blue eyes were so dull there seemed to be a film obscuring them.

He looked up at the windows of his apartment and shook his head. Who was waiting up there for him this time? Moretti—with a gang of hired gunsels? Or maybe Munoz's cutthroats? Or . . .?

He sighed deeply, too utterly tired even to explore the possibilities.

And, in the fifth flood hallway, as he approached his door, he staggered wearily, and his fingers scratched frantically at the wall to hold himself upright. Even the vibrant hands, ordinarily so precise in their every movement, fumbled as they inserted the key into the lock.

The door swung open. He stood there on the threshold, leaning against the jamb. And suddenly knew that there, in the darkness, someone was waiting for him. He could feel a presence. His flesh crawled with fear. But he stood there, too frightened to enter, yet without the strength to run away.

Inside, a shape moved slowly, almost imperceptibly in the blackness. His nerves seemed to twang like guitar strings as they screamed their warning of danger. His heart sank.

He thought: The hell with it. Whatever it is, let it come.

From out of the darkness a voice came. "Pete?" it asked, fearfully.

A sweet voice. A voice with music in it. He should have been overjoyed to hear it. But now, it seemed to rouse no special elation in him.

"Pete . . ." The voice was clearer now, more confident. A switch clicked. Light radiated suddenly from the lamp on the end table.

"I thought you would never come, Pete." Juanita Toy's gravely exquisite face was alight with pleasure at the sight of him. Her wonderful green eyes were luminous with joy.

He forced a mechanical smile and started into the room, swinging the door softly shut behind him. She went to him and curled her arms around his neck. She pulled his head down. Her lips touched his lightly.

But, halfway through the embrace, his fatigue seemed to leave him. His arms tightened around her. He pulled her to him hungrily. The kiss flamed up into a thing of passion.

Finally, she pulled herself away. Concern clouded the happiness in her luminous green eyes. "What happened," she asked softly, "with the police?"

He shrugged. "I insisted it was self-defense."

"It was," she said, with quick loyalty.

"They were reluctant to accept my point of view," he said dryly.

"But they did?"

"Finally."

"I knew you would convince them." She frowned. "If only you had let *me* stay—"

He stopped her by putting the flat of his palm across her mouth. "My lawyer," he explained, "was more helpful than you would have been."

"Perhaps so," she admitted grudgingly, from behind his hand. She kissed the palm, took it between both her own hands. "You are cold," she said softly.

"Tired, too."

She drew him to the couch, sat down beside him. His arm went around her. She leaned back, her head nestled comfortably in the hollow of his shoulder.

They sat in silence for several minutes. His hands were quiet, his face relaxed. Peace seemed to flow over him in waves, lulling him.

The spell was broken by her sudden shudder. He looked down at her inquiringly.

Her eyes had fixed on the center of the rug. He followed her gaze, recognized the ominous dark spot that had attracted her attention.

"Ramon?" he asked gently.

She shivered, nodded.

"He's gone now." Hunter's voice was soft, soothing. "He'll never bother you again."

"No." And now the music in the wonderful voice was melancholy. "Never."

137

"You feared him?"

Again, the reminiscent shudder. She looked up at him, her eyes dark with the memory of terror. "He was evil," she said.

"Evil?" He repeated the word, pondered it. In the quiet of this now-safe room, he found it strange.

But his thoughts went back to that horrible moment, earlier this evening, when he had realized he was about to die. Once more, he could see the fierce triumph blazing bright in the yellow eyes of the young Chinese. And, for a fleeting second, he could even feel the deep defeat with which he had resigned himself to the certainty of impending death.

He knew he would relive that moment many times in the years to come.

He sighed. "I'm glad he's dead."

She said nothing, only snuggled even deeper into the comfort of the niche she had found.

He waited a while, then said, "I wish you would tell me about it."

A frown seamed the smoothness of her brow. "Tell you about it?" she repeated.

"*La calavera de plata.*"

"Oh." Her face brightened again. "Is that not wonderful?"

"Wonderful?"

"That just being with you I could forget all about it." She turned to him. "Yes, Pete, I shall be most happy to tell you the whole story. You are quite sure you are not too tired to listen?"

His face was quite relaxed now. The belated peace had

almost, but not quite, removed all the ravages of this evening. He smiled, and the softness spread even into his usually cold eyes and warmed them.

"I could listen to you forever," he said simply.

She pressed his hand to her lips. "Pete," she asked abruptly, "do you know how a volcano is born?"

"At this hour of the night?" he laughed. "Good Lord, no."

"It is a very miraculous thing," she said soberly.

"I don't doubt it. But what has it to do—?"

"Everything."

He eyed her curiously. It took a moment before he realized that she was deadly serious. He leaned back and closed his eyes.

"I think you'd better tell this one in your own way," he said.

She nodded. "The birth of a volcano, Peter mio," she began, "is an awe-inspiring thing, even to one who understands just what is happening. To the poor uneducated savages of my own country, when it came to pass before their very eyes only five years ago, it was like an evil miracle, a visitation from the devil himself."

"And wasn't it?" he asked dryly.

"In this case, yes and no. It was during the time of a deadly plague, a disease which was causing many deaths among them. And then, one day, as though to multiply their troubles, a rift suddenly appeared in the ground of their communal cornfield. And evil-smelling sulphurous steam issued up from the ground—'as though the stink came right from the mouth of Hell itself,' the Indians said. The earth itself began to rise."

"Subterranean pressures, eh?"

"Exactly. Within a month the earth had risen more than forty meters high. The rift had widened until it was more than one hundred meters."

"Goodbye, cornfield."

"Worse than that. One of the areas affected was an old burial ground, an ancient cemetery they had always regarded as sacred. Now, old bones began to turn up. The Indians took it as a sign of the wrath of God."

"I shouldn't wonder."

"One day, the earth began to shake and, in the cemetery, an old idol was uncovered. Or rather, the head of an idol—fabricated of a metal they had never seen before."

"*La calavera de plata?*"

"Exactly. Only it was not silver."

"Platinum?"

"Yes."

He frowned. "I didn't know there were any platinum mines down there."

"There aren't." She smiled at him appreciatively. "That's why the anthropologists and the archeologists were so excited when they saw the idol. They began to theorize that it must have come from Siberia across—" She broke off. "But that is a story for another day, Pete."

"Right. Let's finish today's."

"On the day when the earth shook and the skull was uncovered, still another miracle occurred, although the Indians did not know it was happening."

"And that was?"

140

"Rafael De Sola arrived to help them."

"De Sola . . .?" He groped in his memory.

"Ricardo's father."

"Ricardo—your fiance."

She blushed, lifted her eyes to his. "My former fiance."

He patted her hand. "We'll have to talk that over another time."

"Whenever you say, Pete." The green eyes met his without reservation.

"Not now, at any rate. Tell me—what was so important about the arrival of De Sola?"

"He was a doctor. And he had penicillin."

"So he began shooting them full of antibiotics and the plague subsided, is that it?"

"Just about. And, since he had arrived the same day the skull was discovered, they decided that the skull was a holy emblem, a power for good. They built a shrine for it and they enthroned it."

"This De Sola—he went on to become the boss of your country?"

"The Indians worshipped him. He had only to imply that he would accept the leadership when there was a spontaneous uprising through the nation. The tide was irresistible."

"As simple as that, eh?"

"Simpler even. One day, he was an unknown doctor; the next, they had made him their dictator."

"And everyone lived happily ever after."

"Until it disappeared . . ."

"*La calavera de plata?*"

"Yes."

He sat up. "Which takes us out of the realm of ancient history and into the area of today. Who has the skull?"

"I do not know."

"Well, dammit, who took it?"

She opened her beautifully formed hands in a gesture of emptiness. "Nobody knows."

"But you think it's here in New York?"

"It must be."

He touched a quick finger to her softly rounded chin, lifted her face so he could look into her eyes. "And if it can't be found, then what?"

"There will be unrest. It is sacred to the Indians."

"If it should be found—they will follow whoever has it?"

She hesitated. "I . . . think so."

He grimaced. "All of which makes it a valuable piece of property."

She nodded.

He bent, kissed her lightly. "And to think," he said, "that I've already sold it to two different people." And, in answer to her puzzled frown, explained his negotiations with Shackleford and Moretti.

"Then *you* have it?" she asked.

"No."

"But how can you—"

"I don't know." His grin was devilish. "But I will, somehow."

She looked up at him, her face softly coquettish now. "And when you do get it, Pete, will you sell it to one of them?"

"No."

"Then what?"

"Give it to you, baby."

"Will you, Pete? Will you really?"

"Of course," he said promptly. "We're partners, aren't we?"

"Yes," she said fervently. "Partners."

"Then let's have a drink on it."

He rose suddenly and went to the liquor cabinet, removed a bottle. "Just sit tight while I get us some ice." He disappeared into the kitchenette, whistling softly to himself.

When he came back, the place where she had been sitting was empty. Immediately, he stiffened. He looked toward the door, half certain she had left.

The sound of water running in the bathroom sink reached him. He shrugged and relaxed, busied himself with the mixing of the drinks.

The bathroom door opened. He heard her footsteps approach. He turned, a glass in each hand, one extended toward her.

It was a gesture that broke off before it was finished. Instead, at the sight of her, his eyebrows climbed halfway up his forehead.

"Oh, baby," he said dreamily, "what you do to me!"

Because this wasn't the demure remote Oriental princess who'd been sitting sedately on the sofa with him.

In place of the modest, severely cut suit, she now wore a filmy negligee. And, in the wonderful green eyes, there now burned a bold challenge.

He surveyed her hungrily. His eyes seemed to devour

143

her . . . The thin lips curled away from his teeth into a grin that showed sharp wolfish teeth.

Quite suddenly, he found himself thinking of last night . . . of the warmth of her body when he had held it hard against his . . . of the softness of her naked flesh to his touch . . . of the torrid fervor of her embrace.

He whistled softly. "Oh, baby—my brain is beginning to boil."

The wonderful green eyes seemed to grow clouded. "I . . . displease you, Pete?"

Again, his eyes surveyed the miniature perfection of her. The wicked grin curved the thin lips wolfishly. "Far from it."

"Then what is wrong?"

"Hell, nothing." He handed her the drink he had prepared, lifted his own high in a toast. "Let's drink to how *right* everything is."

She said, slowly, "I do not understand."

"Don't try to." He took the glass to his lips. "To us, Juanita." He drained it off.

She hesitated, still puzzled, looking from him to the glass in her hand, finally smiled her dazzling smile. "To us," she repeated. She drank.

He began to talk swiftly, mechanically, as if he was using words to fill a vacuum. "I have the feeling," he said, "that we ought to make some sort of melodramatic gesture. Like maybe cracking these glasses on the bar."

He reached for her glass. She was frowning down at its rim. He took it from her. His eyes were fixed on her face now, as if they were looking for something to appear there.

He went on talking. "But frankly, I can't afford it. And the housekeeper—" He turned, put the glasses down "—would have a fit."

She said, "Pete, something has happened." Her voice was frightened.

His eyes never left her face. "Happened?" he asked. "Nothing's happened yet, Juanita." He took her hand, led her to the sofa. She suffered herself to follow, puppet-like, her eyes wide, her lips half parted in bewilderment.

He pulled her down beside him. She made as if to rise. He seized both her shoulders in a firm grasp. "Let's talk about the skull," he said quickly. "About the money it will bring us."

His eyes maintained their careful scrutiny. They were anxious now, as if something that should have happened was being delayed.

She brushed a troubled wavering hand across her eyes. "Peter," she asked, piteously, "what is happening to me?"

"All the millions we'll have." He held her firmly.

She tried to pull away. She said, thickly, "Pete, I feel sh—sick."

He said, soothingly, "Relax, Juanita. Relax."

She struggled desperately against the restraint of his grip. Finally, he released her. Unsteadily, she got to her feet. Her face was deathly pale; her breast heaved as she fought to breathe.

". . . have you done . . . t'me . . .?" Her tongue was a thick unwieldly thing in her mouth. She tried to move toward the door, could no longer control her limbs. She staggered against the gray chair.

He watched her tensely now. The desperation of her

struggle seemed to have communicated itself to him. His face was haggard. Lines of pain bit their way deep into his forehead.

She began to move again, talking almost incoherently, her words an all but unintelligible babble.

". . . . God . . . drugged . . . God . . ." She stumbled, collapsed to her knees. She shook her head, then pushed her hands hard against the floor in an effort to lift her body.

He went to her side quickly, stood above her without touching her. She fought hard, came half erect, gasping, one hand clutching at her throat.

But suddenly, the battle was too much for her. Her body went slack. She surrendered to the engulfing unconsciousness, began to pitch forward.

His quick hands darted out, caught her, held her so that she did not fall. With effortless gentleness, he lifted her in his arms.

He stood there for a moment, holding the unconscious girl. His eyes, ineffably tender now, fixed on her pale face.

He thought: Aren't you the great one, Hunter. Next, you'll be slugging newborn babies!

His face mirrored the ache in his heart. Abruptly, he bent, touched his lips to the girl's half-parted lips.

Half aloud, he said, "Sorry, baby."

It came out like a groan.

15

HE CARRIED her inside, lowered her gently to the bed. There was no sign of the wracking struggle on her face. She lay there, the delicately carved features composed now, the beautiful mouth serene. It was as if she had merely fallen asleep.

The clock beside the bed said eight. A watery morning light filtered in through the blinds. He stood there, staring down at her, his face haggard, devil-driven, his hands curved like talons, tense. Once he shuddered, as if horrified by what he had done. Then, like a man breaking a hypnotic spell, he shook his head violently.

He squared his shoulders and turned away. He still had a big job ahead of him.

He went directly to her handbag, which still stood on the night table where she had left it. His precise knowing hands riffled through its contents, extracted a key ring with several keys on it, as well as the yellow claim check he had seen the night before.

The skies were ominous, the daylight leaden and sickly, when he emerged from the house carrying a small overnight bag. The numbing fatigue which had haunted

147

him earlier still etched its lines in his face. But now, there was a new look in his eyes, the feverish fire of the hunter reacting to the tension of the chase. He hailed a passing cab, directed its driver to take him to the Garland Hotel.

Once there, he went boldly up to her suite and let himself in with one of the keys on the ring he had taken from her purse. The rooms themselves were stripped bare, completely devoid of any ornament that might have suggested her presence. Three modish suitcases, packed and locked, stood beside the sofa.

Hunter acted completely unsurprised. As though this were merely what he had expected, he went directly to them, bent and, with the other keys on the ring, unlocked them one by one.

Now, the slim eager fingers again performed their precise probing routine, examining the neatly folded clothing thoroughly, feeling walls and linings sensitively until, in the third and largest of the bags, they came upon what they had been seeking. It was a small object, no more than ten inches in length, and it had been casually wrapped in a soft cashmere sweater of subtlest green.

He paused before unwrapping it, his nostrils suddenly aware of the delicate fragrance of Juanita Toy herself emanating from the garment. Again, the sharp lancet of pain sliced deep into his haggard features at the thought of her. He closed his eyes against the haunting image of her face.

But now the impatient hands insisted. They had found their quarry and they would not be denied. Almost as if revolting against the sentimentality of the mind that controlled them, they were anxiously plucking at the delicate wool, peeling away the concealing layers of filmy fabric until, at long last, the coveted statuette beneath was unveiled.

There was a sharp hiss as he sucked his breath. He stared down at it. A wave of disappointment swept over him.

Was this what they had been killing each other for—this plain, ugly, Mongolian-featured head, so rudely sculptured of tin? A sense of frustration welled up in him, so strong he felt like crying—a child who had awakened on Christmas Day to discover that Santa Claus had not come.

This drab piece of dross—was this *la calavera de plata?*

But, even as his hands moved, one of the eyes, which had seemed so dull to him, captured a ray of light, imprisoned it and fractured it into a thousand dancing flecks of fire. The effect was so utterly dazzling that it literally took his breath away.

Now, his examination of the skull was almost reverent. The dull metal, it came to him, was not tin at all, but platinum—many, many times more valuable than its equivalent weight of gold. And those eyes, which had at first seemed a drab paste, were actually huge, priceless diamonds. He let out his breath in a long slow sigh.

The delicate fingers turned it over now, examined it like a surgeon probing for the malignancy beneath the surface of the skin. For this rude ugly statuette had a history of blood. Men had killed each other for it—would perhaps do so again.

149

Holding it in his hands, he began to feel the magnetic force of it. It meant *power*—a force that could literally move a nation, will millions of human beings into action. He shook his head sadly, began to wrap it again in the soft cashmere which had been its envelope.

When he had finished, he put it into the small bag he had brought with him, then closed and re-locked Juanita Toy's suitcases. At the doorway he paused for one last look before he left, then nodded, satisfied that, with the exception of what he had taken away in the bag, everything was as he had found it.

The clerk at the parcel room in Pennsylvania Station didn't even look up when Peter Hunter presented the yellow claim check which had so recently resided in Juanita Toy's purse. To him, faces were meaningless. The only things that mattered were the little squares of colored cardboard that he stared at through his thick, dirty-lensed spectacles. And people merely represented packages stored away in the labyrinth of cubbyholes behind him.

It wasn't until Hunter said pleasantly, "I just want to get something out of it," that the clerk looked up at his customer.

Then he said, irritatedly, "Don't make no difference, pal. If I get the item, you gotta pay on it."

Hunter smiled. "Okay," he said. He handed the man a five-dollar bill. "Take it out of that."

The clerk turned the claim check over, tugged at a

thick untidy mustache. "This item been here a long time already. Two weeks."

"That's right," Hunter admitted. "I just want to take something out of it, then you can put it back. Just so I get the same check."

The clerk peered out at him through the thick dirty lenses. "Same check?"

"That's right: same check."

Probably, if Hunter had said nothing at all, he would have been given the same yellow square of cardboard as a matter of course. But to have such a request voiced was a disturbance of routine. And, in his irritation, the man behind the counter elected to make an issue of it.

"The *same* check, pal? What's so damn important about the same check? What if I give ya another check? You ain't gonna leave the item with me? You gonna spite me and take it to a competitor? Grand Central Station is gonna get your business from now on, maybe?"

Hunter's eyes frowned, even as the lips continued to form their patient smile. "You believe in numerology?" he asked.

"Numerology? I never even heard of it. Biology, I know about. Geology—"

"Numbers," Hunter broke in quickly. "They're important to me."

"Oh." The clerk's smile was superior. "Lucky numbers, ya mean? Ya superstitious about 'em?"

"Aren't you?"

"*Me!*" The eyes behind the dirty lenses laughed. "Not me, pal. Why—" he groped for words to express his disdain "—why, thirteen is my *lucky* number."

Quietly, Hunter laid a bill on the counter. "How about ten?"

The half-obscured eyes glinted. "No strings?"

"Just the same check, that's all."

"Tell ya the truth, pal," the clerk leaned forward, smiling broadly as he picked up the money, "I always had a weakness for ten, too." He winked knowingly. "I'll get the item for ya right away."

"Thanks."

"Anything ya want, ya can do with it."

The "item" turned out to be a tan cowhide Gladstone bag. Hunter searched through it until he found a small, paper-wrapped package about as large as the one he had taken from Juanita Toy's suitcase at the Garland Hotel. This he laid to one side, then returned the bag to the clerk. The clerk smiled, issued the same yellow parcel check to him.

Then, clutching the package under his arm, he went to the lower level of the station, inserted a dime into one of the overnight lockers and, when it opened, stowed away the bag he had brought with him from his own apartment. That done, he went back to Juanita Toy's suite at the Garland Hotel, still carrying the paper-wrapped package he had taken from the Gladstone at the checkroom.

By the time he returned to his own home, it was ten o'clock in the morning. Juanita Toy was still sleeping so calmly that it seemed she hadn't even moved. He looked down at her and felt the hot shame flood into his cheeks.

He took her pulse briefly, not because it was necessary,

but in response to some fleeting need to do something for her. Then, he crossed to her handbag and restored the claim check and key ring he had taken earlier.

He went into the kitchenette, set about making himself breakfast. Hungrily, he wolfed down bacon and eggs, drank two cups of coffee, bitter and black.

Those things done, he felt and looked much better. It would have been hard to guess, from his face, that he had slept only about four hours in the last forty-eight.

Quickly, he washed the dishes, returned them to the cupboard. He went into the living room, moved directly to the telephone and dialed a number.

To the voice that replied at the other end, he said: "Put Mr. Moretti on, please."

At twenty-five minutes past ten that morning, Frankie Moretti was awakened by a gentle tugging at his shoulder. He rolled over in bed, reached out a bare, tanned arm and looked at the diamond-studded wrist watch that lay on the night table.

When he saw the time, he lifted his head angrily. "How many times have I told you—"

The Filipino houseboy smiled apologetically as he interrupted. "I sorry, sah. A Mr. Hunter on the telephone. He say very important."

"Hunter, eh?" Moretti's scowl changed to a sleek smile. "That's different. Tell 'im I'll be right there."

He threw the covers off and stepped out of the bed. On his way to the window, he stopped to study the reflection of his naked body in the mirror. Eyes fixed on the glass, he stretched out his arms and executed two deep knee bends. He went to the window, opened it wide and did deep breathing exercises for one full minute. On his way to the telephone, he again stopped to examine himself as he passed before the mirror.

He picked up the receiver. "Yes, doll?"

Hunter's voice was crisp, yet surcharged with tension. "You still want that ornament, Moretti?"

"I still want it, doll. Real bad."

"How bad?"

"So bad I can taste it."

"Twenty-five G's bad?"

"I don't go back on my word, doll."

"All right, Moretti. In an hour—come to my house alone and get it. And don't forget to bring a certified check for the dough."

"Now, wait a minute—"

"Don't haggle with me, Moretti," Hunter broke in harshly. "And don't *doll* me, either. If you want it, come and get it. And don't forget—bring that check."

The phone disconnected.

Frankie Moretti frowned as he stared down at the dead instrument. Who in hell did that Hunter punk think he was, passing out orders that way? Why, he had half a mind to send Rocky—

The thought broke off as he remembered how Rocky had been handled yesterday. Again, Moretti frowned. But then, just as suddenly, the frown turned into the sleek satisfied smile.

So, the punk had the loot and was ready to deal for it, eh? And from what that old fool, Shackleford, had said, the gizmo ought to be worth at least three hundred G's. Of course, what with the government restrictions on platinum, he'd have to take it to the black market.

Still, that shouldn't be too hard . . .

He went back to the mirror, turned this way and that before it, searching the glass for flaws in his body. He lifted his arm and rotated it, pleased with the rippling of muscle induced by the motion.

Then, still smiling sleekly, he padded off to take his shower.

At ten twenty-five that morning, Phineas T. Shackleford had been awake and thinking hard for almost three-quarters of an hour. To be specific, he had been pondering the problem of the missing Ramon.

Not that Shackleford felt an emotional loss at the absence of the young Chinese. Far from it. But he would have liked to know what had happened at Peter Hunter's house last night. For a while, he had toyed with the possibility of calling Peter Hunter and asking him point blank. Ultimately, though, he had put the idea aside. It was not like Mr. Shackleford to do anything point blank.

He realized, of course, that it was quite likely that Ramon was dead. If the Chinese, in spite of the warning that he, Shackleford, had telephoned after Hunter's departure, had persisted in staying in the apartment long enough to meet the latter, then a violent collision must certainly have ensued. Quite probably, only one of them had emerged alive. And, since Ramon had failed to return, it seemed a safe assumption that the survivor had not been he.

Shackleford sighed. He would miss Ramon. In spite of his surliness, the Chinese had been useful.

So, Ramon was dead. Again, the lean cadaverous old man mourned his servant's passing with a long expiration of breath. Then, his obeisance to the dear departed paid, he crossed to the telephone and directed room service to bring him his breakfast.

And, as Phineas Shackleford detailed it, it was to be an excellent breakfast . . .

It was shortly thereafter, at ten thirty-five to be precise, while he was waiting for his morning meal to be brought up, that the telephone rang. He lifted the receiver and, even before he could identify himself, the voice at the other end snapped: "Shackleford—this is Peter Hunter."

Peter Hunter! He felt a thrill shoot through his aged veins.

A thought stopped him: What of Ramon? But he merely said, "Delighted to hear from you, Mr. Hunter."

"Your boy's in the morgue."

Again, Phineas sighed. His suspicions, alas, had been only too well founded. He said, "Congratulations, Mr. Hunter."

"Thanks."

"I take it you were responsible for his demise."

Hunter hesitated. "In a way."

"My compliments, sir. Ramon was a formidable adversary."

"That's not why I called."

"No?" Again, the old man felt a thrill of elation. "Is it then about the—"

"Yes. *La calavera de plata.*"

"*Ah!*" He could not contain himself. Then, guardedly: "You have it?"

"Yes. You still interested?"

"*Interested!* My dear fellow—"

"Good. Be at my apartment in half an hour."

"At your apartment—"

"I'm unloading it."

"Unloading it? You mean you are prepared to turn it over—"

"Yes."

"Excellent. I shall—" The old man broke off, stared at the receiver. It was dead. Hunter had disconnected.

What a strange abrupt young man, this Hunter. *Unloading* it, he had said. That would mean that, at this very moment, the precious idol was in Hunter's apartment. Like a ripe fruit, waiting to be plucked.

Ah, if only Ramon were here!

Again, he sighed at his loss. Still, perhaps he didn't need Ramon . . . perhaps he could accomplish it alone. The youthful fire that flared up in Shackleford's black eyes belied the evidence of advanced years.

But quickly, it died away. No, that Hunter fellow was really too formidable. Nor would it be easy to deceive him.

With a philosophical shrug, Phineas Shackleford decided to accept the inevitable. After all, half a loaf was better than none.

He chuckled. Especially, he thought, since he was actually contributing nothing to the venture. Anyone holding the idol the poor benighted Indians had endowed with divinity could conduct the negotiations with De Sola.

Half a loaf it would be then.

The old swindler's eyes twinkled as another thought struck him. Mr. Peter Hunter would hardly be in a position to see the full loaf before it had been bisected. The chances were, therefore, that his half would be considerably inferior to Phineas Shackleford's half.

A discreet knock at the door interrupted his musings. He opened it to admit the waiter with the cart bearing his breakfast. Phineas bent over it, lifted covers from casserole dishes and sniffed appreciatively.

Half a loaf, he thought—and sat down to eat.

16

IT WAS eleven forty-five now, but the day was as dark as it had been at dawn. In the somber confines of the small apartment nerves had become strained, tautened close to the breaking point.

Frankie Moretti broke the heavy silence. "Okay, doll," he said unpleasantly, "you got me here. I don't like how you did it—but I'm here." He leaned his trim form forward in the gray chair, looking like a sleek well-muscled cat about to spring. "Now—I want what I come for."

"After we're all here, Moretti," Hunter snapped.

"All, doll? Who else?"

"I can scarcely see any necessity for being precipitate." Excitement had caused Phineas Shackleford's rasping voice to rise an octave above its natural register. "Can't we—er—merely relax and enjoy Mr. Hunter's hospitality?"

Moretti turned toward him. "And what's this creep doin' here?" he asked Hunter.

"I invited him."

"I don't want him, doll."

"I do."

Moretti stabbed a glance at the jeweled watch on his wrist. "I ain't waiting much longer, doll."

Hunter shrugged indifference to the implied threat. Shackleford cleared his throat to make an announcement. The sound was pitched so high it came out like the whir of a cricket.

"As to the personage we are awaiting," he said, "if I may offer a conjecture . . ." The bright black eyes burned young in the seamed old face.

Hunter said, smiling, "Conjecture away."

Before the old man could voice his guess, there was a small distinct sound somewhere in the apartment. Moretti jumped from his chair as though shot from the mouth of a cannon. As if by magic, an automatic now glowered in his right hand.

"What the hell is *that*, doll?"

"That?" Hunter asked.

With meaningful menace, Moretti gestured toward his host with the weapon. "Don't double-talk me, doll. I heard something. You heard it. The creep heard it. Now—what the hell was it?"

Shackleford rubbed a bony finger along the long spade-like projection of his jaw. "That, Mr. Moretti, in your own argot, is a doll. A girl doll, unless I'm mistaken. And, as I was about to conjecture, it is none other than Miss Juanita Toy."

Hunter rose quickly, turned toward the bedroom. "I'll bring her right out," he said.

"Play it clean, doll," Moretti warned. "Play it clean." He punctuated his nervousness with little jab-like motions of the automatic. "I'm getting itchy."

She had just finished searching through her purse. At the sound of his entry, she snapped the catch shut and turned. Her wonderful sea-green eyes opened wide at the sight of him. Doubt shadowed their lustrous depths.

"Pete!" His name burst from her lips almost like a sob.

She went to him and her arms embraced him hard. He held her tight. She clung to him for a moment, then stepped back from him. The wonderful green eyes tried hard to read something in the mask that was his face.

She said: "Pete, last night . . ."

He stopped her with a quick motion of his excited hands. "Forget it," he said brusquely. "Forget last night." His face became more mask-like than ever.

"But you drugged me. Why, Pete? Why?"

The expressive hands clenched, then opened in an empty gesture. "There were . . . things to do."

"Things, Pete? What things?"

"It's a long story, princess. Much too long for now. Besides, we have guests waiting."

"Guests?" The lovely green eyes clouded, narrowed. A single sharp frowning line marred the clear expanse of her flawless brow. "What kind of guests?"

"A Mr. Moretti. A Mr. Shackleford."

She gasped audibly. "Them!"

"On business."

"Business? What business?"

"They've come to buy something from us."

"But my people—"

A thin quick finger darted to her lips, abruptly dammed

the flow of her words. He said, lightly, "Let's not keep them waiting."

"But I—"

This time it was his lips that stopped her. He had meant it to be nothing more than a carefree gesture. But something happened to his plans. Before he knew it, his arms had tightened around her. The casual embrace had ignited passion.

Reluctantly, he recalled his purpose, broke away from her. She clung to him when they parted, speaking breathlessly. "I'm so frightened, Pete," she said. "So terribly, terribly frightened."

He said, simply: "So am I."

Again, the incredibly green eyes searched his face. But this time the doubt in them turned to wonder. "You really *are* frightened," she said unbelievingly. "Even more than I am, I think."

His smile was rueful, uncertain. "Let's not keep our guests waiting," he said.

As he turned away, the wonder in her face gave way to an expression of ineffable pity. She reached out a hand to stop him, but it was too late.

He was gone . . .

Hunter's heart went into his throat when she came into the living room. She entered like a personage of royalty, a remotely beautiful queen. Her acknowledgement of the introduction to Moretti was a regal inclination of her head: her dismissal of Shackleford a disdainful nod.

Peter Hunter swallowed hard at the unswallowable lump as he watched her. A look of hunger came into his eyes. They seemed to devour her. And they held something more than hunger: they held pain, too. Pain and the dread of imminent loss.

He looked like someone who knew he was soon to be deprived of something unutterably precious.

She seated herself, pointedly taking the chair farthest from him. The hurt in his eyes deepened at the slight. When they all looked at him, his eyes went to her. For a moment, he seemed to waver, seemed about to change his mind. But then the thin lips clamped together resolutely, the set of his mouth firmed.

He said, glancing around the small circle, "Now that we're all here—"

"I want that loot, doll."

Hunter ignored the gangster. "We are all interested in—"

"If I may interrupt, Mr. Hunter." This time it was Shackleford.

Hunter sighed, shrugged.

The thin old man turned to Moretti. "May I inquire— you have your weapon in readiness, sir?"

"What's it to you?"

"May I suggest that you concentrate your attention on Miss Toy?"

Moretti started to snort contempt, then met the glance of the black eyes in the old seamed face. Seeing the deadly seriousness there, he shook his head wonderingly.

He turned his eyes to Juanita Toy. She met the inspection with a cold lift of her chin. Experimentally, Moretti's fingers moved across his chest toward the holster in his left armpit.

Shackleford nodded approval of the gangster's precaution. "She is quite the most dangerous of us all, I assure you." He turned to Hunter again. "And you, sir—I trust you have had the forethought to assure yourself that she is not armed. She is, as I've warned you, quite a deadly shot."

Hunter smiled grimly. "I've already had proof of that."

Juanita Toy's face remained regally contemptuous. The only sign of tension was a slight dilation of the nostrils, almost like a jungle cat scenting danger.

Still talking to Phineas Shackleford, Hunter said: "It was she who killed your man last night, y'know." He spoke of the Chinese girl as if she weren't even there.

"Ramon?"

"Yes. Right here."

"But I thought you—"

"Not I—she." He turned to Juanita. "I suppose I should feel flattered, shouldn't I?"

The pallor of her face endowed her with a certain icy remoteness—almost a star-like quality. The wonderful green eyes met his wordlessly.

He said: "Your own brother, too."

She broke her silence. Her voice was soft, full of a sad music. She said, "I love you, Pete." As if that was explanation enough.

He winced as though she'd struck him. Gritting his teeth he went on. "He was your brother, wasn't he?" He asked the question breathlessly, fearing the horror of the answer.

The wonderful green eyes bored into his. She said, "Yes." It was as if they were alone in the room.

"And you killed him."

With quiet defiance: "Yes."

"Because you couldn't control him any longer."

"For you."

"For *me!*"

"Why else?"

She squared her shoulders. The small, beautifully rounded breasts outlined themselves against the thinness of her blouse. The wonderful green eyes lighted up.

"It was the only way I could save you. I killed him because I love you."

He tried to stare her down but, in the combat of wills, it was he who weakened first. He cast his eyes down and, for a moment, one quick hand covered his face.

She said, "In another second he'd have killed you. I shot him from the door."

"Then changed the guns so I'd think he'd been killed in the struggle between us."

She didn't answer.

"I would have thought so, too," he went on, "but the wound in his head had no powder burns. That's why Grogan thought my story about a struggle wah a phoney."

He waited for her to speak but she ignored him. Finally, he said, "And you've had the idol all the time, haven't you?"

"No."

"Then why did Shackleford—"

"Think you had it, Mr. Hunter?" the old man finished. "Because I saw her bring it to you. I was following her that day. She was carrying a package of just the right size. I naturally assumed that she had entrusted it to you for safe-keeping."

"But it was an empty package." Hunter smiled admiringly. "And, somewhere between the time you lost sight of her when she entered the building and I first saw her in my office, she merely disposed of an already empty package. And everyone was sure she'd left it with me."

"But I did not have it," she insisted quietly.

"What about now—do you have it now?" he persisted.

Her smile was a mocking, teasing thing.

He shrugged. "I already know the answer," he said.

Her smile vanished.

Moretti said, quite abruptly: "The hell with all this chin music. I come here for the loot and I want it."

"You have the check?" Hunter asked.

He patted his breast pocket. "Right here, doll."

Hunter turned to Juanita. "Mr. Moretti has a certified check for twenty-five thousand dollars. You will give him the silver skull for it."

"No, Pete, I will not." She said simply, but firmly.

"You're lucky to get even that much."

"It isn't the money," she said stubbornly. "It is my people—"

"Your people!" He pounced on the word like a panther. "A crooked-tongued lie — your people. The bloody butchers you've been spying for—are *they* your people?"

Her wonderful green eyes flashed sparks. A sudden surge of anger crimsoned her cheeks. The flush in her face made her radiantly beautiful.

Her head lifted higher than ever, she said, "Pete, I

have to talk to you—alone."

He shook his head.

"I must," she insisted.

"It's useless."

She crossed the room to him, her eyes never leaving his. He watched her, hypnotized.

"If you love me, Peter . . ."

"You'll let her deceive you and cheat you and sacrifice you, Mr. Hunter," Shackleford finished dryly.

Hunter turned to him angrily. As if reacting to the old man's sarcasm, he turned without a word and led her into the bedroom.

Phineas Shackleford licked his lips as he watched them leave.

When the door had closed behind them, Peter Hunter turned to her, began to speak quickly. The words poured out as though he felt he had to speak first, as though he feared to let her take the offensive.

"All right," he said roughly, "let's admit one thing. I love you. But it doesn't mean a goddam thing as far as this is concerned."

"But it is everything, Pete. Everything."

"Nothing. Not a goddam thing. Even if you love me—"

"But I do. I do."

"It doesn't make a damn bit of difference. You're going with Moretti. You'll take his check and cash it. And, once you've gotten the money you'll give him the skull. Then, you'll get the hell out of the country."

"But where, Pete? Where will I go?"

"Where had you planned to go?" he demanded savagely. "You must know—you've planned the whole thing from the beginning, haven't you?"

Her face relaxed, as if she were dropping a mask. "Yes," she said, and her voice had a breathless, little-girl-lost quality. "I planned it all. I'm not going to lie any more. I did plan it, though," and here a wry bitterness tinged her words, "not quite like this."

The confession seemed to arouse him even further. "What did you plan? To have me fall in love with you? To use me to front for you? Be a fall guy for your traps? A sucker for your lies?" He seized her by the shoulders. The fingers of steel bit so viciously into her flesh that she winced. "Have you ever told me the truth? Even once?"

The wonderful green eyes met his, held them. She said, so softly it was barely audible, "Yes. Once."

"And when was that?"

The voice was sad. "When I said I loved you."

His cold blue eyes searched her face, seemed to devour it hungrily. The excited hands clamped hard on her arms again. "If I could believe that."

"You must."

"I don't."

"How can I prove it to you?"

"You can't."

"But I must. I must!" Desperately, her eyes circled the room as though seeking some evidence to prove what she said. Suddenly, she said: "Peter—if I gave it to you . . ."

"Gave me—"

"*La calavera de plata*. The silver skull. If I said: 'Here

it is—to prove I really love you. Take it. Without conditions . . ." She groped for words. "No strings attached."

Fascinated, he watched the play of emotion across the screen of her face. His icy blue eyes softened. "You'd do that? You'd actually do that?"

"Yes."

"Give up all that money?"

"Gladly."

"Risk offending those who have hired you?"

"For you—yes."

"De Sola would pay millions," he reminded her.

She laughed, the tuneful tinkle of tiny bells. "De Sola's millions—poof!"

Laughing with her, he said, "I can't believe you."

"I'll prove it."

"All right: prove it."

"I'll tell you where it is and how to get it. And I'll wait at the hotel until you have returned with it."

His blue eyes never left her face. There was a look in them that spoke of how anxious he was to believe her. But he said, cautiously, "And what will I do with it after I've gotten it?"

Her delighted smile became a rueful one. "You will probably call that implacable Mr. Matthews of your State Department. You will tell him what you have. And then—he will come and take it from you."

"And what about you?"

The smile on her face became bright again. She looked like a bright-eyed child playing make-believe. She said: "I will be at the hotel. You will call me and tell me what you have done. And I will hate you for giving it away—

and love you for the strength you have."

"And everyone will live happily ever after?"

"Why not?" The smile was ecstatic now. "Shall we do it, Pete? Shall we?"

Again, his eyes searched her face. His hands lifted, started to go out to her in a hesitant hunger.

As though to hasten his decision, she turned away from him, went to her purse and extracted something from it. She put it into his hand, closed his fingers over it.

"What's this?" she asked.

"Take it," she said breathlessly. "With it, you will get the silver skull."

His face relaxed into a smile. His eyes, never leaving her face, softened to a deep sky blue. He said, "Thank you, Juanita."

"I have made you happy, Pete? I am glad."

He opened his hand, looked down at what it held. The blue eyes froze. His face stiffened into an implacable mask. The fingers seemed to wilt, curl up in defeat.

"Is something wrong, Pete?" She spoke quickly, almost ferfully.

"This is it?"

She nodded, her body tense.

An expression of pain crossed his face. He closed his eyes against it. When he spoke, his voice was a harsh, unrecognizable snarl. "No—it can't be done."

She was about to argue with him but the look on his face stilled her words before she could utter them. After a moment, she sighed in slow acceptance of rejection.

"Then it cannot be, Peter mio?" She spoke almost inaudibly into the tense silence.

He did not answer.

"Pete?"

"No." It was final.

She started toward the door, stopped when he spoke to her again.

"Here," he said, "you'd better take this back."

She held out her hand. He returned what she had given him a few minutes before.

The worthless yellow claim check . . .

The two men in the living room eyed Peter Hunter warily when he and Juanita Toy returned. Moretti's automatic was no longer in evidence but the gangster's right hand hovered at his chest, ready to dart in toward the weapon's nest in his armpit should developments demand it. A small muscle in his jaw twitched compulsively, betraying the tension he fought to disguise.

Phineas Shackleford tilted his head to one side in a gesture that was almost birdlike. The excitement sparkling in his jet black eyes made him look like an aged intent crow. He cleared his throat in his own peculiarly strident fashion.

"Mr. Hunter," he said, and his voice was harsh, "I trust you have not succumbed to Miss Toy's not inconsiderable blandishments."

Juanita Toy curled her lip in regal disdain at the old man's sarcasm. Hunter said, flatly, "It's all settled."

Moretti's nervous hand hopped across his chest, closer to the automatic in the shoulder holster. The hot brown eyes narrowed. "Settled how, doll?"

"Miss Toy will turn the silver skull over to you. You will give her the certified check."

"Miss Toy!" Shackleford literally sputtered in anger. *"Miss Toy!"*

Hunter turned to face him.

The old man made no effort to hide his complete contempt. "Mr. Hunter," he said pityingly, "you are an absolute, utter, indescribable fool."

Hunter shrugged.

"Because, Mr. Hunter, if you are of the opinion that Miss Toy will return to share the proceeds of this venture with you, you have reached the heights of naivete."

As if Shackleford hadn't said a word, Juanita Toy arose and went to Peter Hunter. "There is no other way?"

"None."

"My life? My love? You disdain them?" The wonderful green eyes pleaded with him.

He remained silent. His eyes avoided hers. Finally, as though he did not trust his voice, he shook his head mutely. For an instant, she seemed to sag in defeat. But her indomitable will asserted itself. She lifted her head, squared her shoulders and turned to face Moretti.

As though reacting to a command in her eyes, the gangster spoke to Hunter. "Okay, doll," he snapped, "let's get this show on the road. If we're going to promote this deal, let's get it over with."

It was as though Hunter hadn't heard his words. He stared hard at Juanita Toy's back until the Chinese girl turned back to him.

172

Then he said, quietly, "Did you hear the man, princess?"

"I heard him, Pete." Her voice was soft, sad. "I heard him."

The words seemed to hang in the air like a melancholy music.

Hunter said, "Well . . .?"

For a moment, she hesitated, looking from Hunter to Moretti, then quietly, quickly opened the door and left. The gangster got up to follow. Hand across his chest, close to the shoulder holster, he backed out slowly, his eyes vigilant to protect himself from any treachery.

The door closed. The silence of the grave settled down on the room after they left.

After what seemed like centuries, Phineas Shackleford got up and went to the telephone. Peter Hunter watched him wordlessly.

The old man paused as he was about to lift the receiver. He studied the younger man for a long moment, then said:

"Are you aware, Mr. Hunter, that you have just betrayed your country to a foreign power?"

173

17

Grimly, Hunter said: "Put that telephone down."

The old man raised his eyebrows. "Really now, Mr. Hunter, I was merely about to—"

"Call Matthews. You want to get out from under."

"I assure you—"

"To tell him of the gallant effort you made to save an important political symbol—*la calavera de plata*—for your country."

The old man glowered. "And of the traitor who thwarted me."

"Of course, you'll omit the proposition you made me."

"A far better one than you finally accepted," the old man blurted bitterly. "Why, Mr. Hunter, did you even bother to have me here if you intended to dismiss me so carelessly?"

"Because," Hunter's smile was fondly indulgent, "I didn't want you running around loose so you could louse up my arrangements."

"Arrangements! You'll never see Miss Toy again."

Hunter nodded. "I don't expect to."

"Don't expect to!" The old man was amazed.

"Of course not."

"You mean—you want it this way? With her escaping scot free? With all the money?"

"Exactly."

Shock left the old man dumb. Still smiling, Hunter took his arm, led him away from the telephone.

"If it makes you feel any better," he said soothingly, "I spoke to Matthews this morning. He'll be here at two." He glanced down at his watch. "In just an hour, Mr. Shackleford."

"And I suppose," the old man finally asked, "that you're bringing him here so that he can't interfere with your precious arrangements, either."

Hunter nodded admiringly. "You read me like a book."

"So that, while Matthews sits talking with you, your lady love is winging her way out over the ocean."

"The plane for Rotterdam leaves at two-thirty."

"With *la calavera de plata?*"

"No, Moretti will have that. She'll have the money."

"Yes." Shackleford digested the information. "You seem to have thought of everything, Mr. Hunter," he said. "Except one . . ."

"Yes?"

He leaned forward. The aged black eyes blazed into Hunter's. "You're the one who stays behind! What do you say when they accuse you of being a traitor?"

The hour dragged itself by . . . but the man from the State Department did not come. Tensely, Peter Hunter prowled the small apartment. Irritably, he picked up a book, put it down unopened. He went to the window, looked out. The man he awaited was nowhere in sight. He resumed his pacing. The slim nervous fingers curled in upon one another tautly. The thin lips pressed together into a knife-line.

"Could it be, Mr. Hunter," the old man asked, his long eel-like body curled into a chair, "that you have been outguessed?" The idea afforded him inner amusement.

Hunter glared at him, then went to the telephone. He dialed a number. The answering voice told him Mr. Matthews was out. No, it didn't know when he'd be back. Nor where he might be reached. Hunter slapped the instrument down savagely.

Where the hell was Matthews? What was holding him up?

He wanted the damned skull, didn't he?

Then why in hell wasn't he here?

Could it be he'd caught Juanita before she could get away? No, that was impossible. He couldn't have known what was going on.

All right, then—everything was going fine. There was nothing to worry about. The deal would be completed. Juanita would escape.

But—where was Matthews?

For still another hour, he paced up and down the little space, wrestling with his own tortured doubts; alternating between blaming his own stupidity, then reassuring himself. Until, at three o'clock—like a requiem bell signalling the release from struggle—the door chime announced the arrival of the man from the State Department.

176

Grimly, Matthews heard the details of the arrangement that had freed Juanita Toy to make her deal with Moretti. Impassively, he listened to Phineas Shackleford's dramatic denunciation of Hunter as a traitor.

And when the old man had finished, the man from the State Department turned to Peter Hunter. His voice was still soft when he spoke, but his eyes were bright, and hard as diamonds. "I'm here for the whole story, Mr. Hunter."

Hunter's face was haunted now, gray and bloodless. His slim figure seemed defenseless against the other's imposing bulk.

But he shook his head in defiance. "You'll answer some questions for me, first," he insisted.

The big man studied him. The gleaming inscrutable eyes weighed the younger man. He said: "Mr. Hunter, you've run this show just as you've pleased. Thinking of nothing but your own selfish—no, dammit, don't interrupt me—nothing but your own selfish profit. It's time you realized that your country's security's at stake here, that you don't count worth a damn. Now, I'll say it again and for the last time: I want the whole story. And until I get it, I'll answer no questions, make no bargains. Is that clear?"

The words brooked no contradiction. Pleadingly, Hunter's eyes searched the other's face. Piteously, the eloquent hands cupped themselves toward the big man. "I've got to know," he insisted. "Juanita Toy—did she get away?"

"Juanita Toy?" Matthews hesitated. There was something peculiar in the way he inflected the name.

"The Chinese girl."

"She . . . escaped capture." It was heavy, an admission of failure.

As if they sensed there was more to be told, Hunter's icy blue eyes searched the big man's face.

Matthews said sharply: "I want that story, Mr. Hunter. Now."

Hunter shrugged. "What do you want to know?" he asked softly.

"Everything. About Munoz. Shackleford here. Everyone else. The whole story."

"Most of all," somehow Hunter found the strength to offer a tired bitter grin, "about *la calavera de plata.*"

"Ah—the silver skull." The words came out in a sigh. Phineas Shackleford came to life for a moment. "That, most of all, eh, Mr. Matthews?"

There was much to tell . . . Hunter's eyes sought the ceiling while he tried to organize his thoughts.

His mind went to the Chinese girl . . . riding the big silver plane this very moment . . . each successive minute carrying her farther and farther away . . .

But—had she escaped? He couldn't be sure. There was something about the way Matthews had said her name . . .

He swallowed hard. No matter what had happened, he couldn't help her any more. Except that holding this Matthews here now might do some good. The longer he talked, he tried to tell himself, the better it was for Juanita.

He turned to them. "I guess you could say," he began, "that Juanita Toy was the central figure. Everyone thought she had the idol—"

"And did she?"

"She did and she didn't."

"I think," Matthews said, after a moment's thought, "I'd better let you explain that your own way."

Hunter nodded. "She was supposed to marry young De Sola, wasn't she?"

"Yes."

"But Munoz stopped that. Why?"

"He didn't trust her. She'd come from nowhere. He didn't know who she was, or who she was connected with."

Hunter's grin was tight. "He—and you—didn't like the company she kept, either?"

"No."

"The Reds?"

Matthews sighed. He'd covered this ground so many times. "Miss Toy—" he began, then stopped as if the name stuck in his mouth.

Hunter's eyes narrowed. His hands constricted.

Matthews finally said: "Let's just say she ran around with the anti-American element."

"So Munoz broke up the marriage and she disappeared. You people said good riddance until—"

"Until," Matthews admitted grimly, "we found that *la calavera de plata* was also gone from its shrine."

"Whereupon you decided she'd run off with it."

"And didn't she?"

"No."

"How do you know?"

"The way she acted. Playing for time. Fooling Shackle-

179

ford by pretending to bring it to me in a box. Most of all, by not selling it—which she'd certainly have done if she had it."

"Yet, she did sell it to Moretti this morning."

"Yes. But it wasn't she who stole it and brought it to this country."

"Then who did?"

"Who? Well, ask yourself: who *would?* And, there's only one answer. The guy who was in love with her. The guy she was going to marry." He leaned forward to ask the question, his frozen blue eyes riveted to those of Matthews. "Where is this young De Sola? Home? I'll bet not. I'll bet he's in Chicago or L. A. by now—waiting for her to join him."

For once, Matthews' composure broke. "He turned up in Chicago yesterday. How did *you* know that?"

"I didn't."

"Then how—"

"How else? How else could they force his father into letting them get married?"

Shackleford grunted. "Or so she told *him.*"

Hunter ignored the comment, went on to tell of the night he'd saved Juanita from being tortured by her own Red partners because they figured she was playing games with the skull . . . of the telephone call she'd received . . . of her pretense of writing an alleged telegraph message after the other end had obviously disconnected.

"What did that mean?" Matthews asked.

"She'd left a call with the hotel desk to be told when it was twelve-fifteen. I followed her cab. It was on its way to Idlewild Airport."

"To meet De Sola and collect the idol?"

"What else?"

"And you know that happened? He brought it to her?"

"He must have."

"Don't you *know?*"

"No. I didn't go to the airport."

"Feeling the way he did about Miss Toy," Shackleford interjected dryly, "you can readily understand why Mr. Hunter might not relish witnessing such a tender meeting as theirs was apt to be."

Hunter turned baleful eyes on the old man, but said nothing.

Matthews' voice cut into the tension between them. "Let's answer some other questions, Mr. Hunter. First, who killed Munoz?" He hesitated. ". . . Miss Toy?"

Hunter's eyes narrowed. *That pause again. That reluctance to speak the name.*

What did it mean? Was it because she had so thoroughly outwitted him? Or . . .

Hunter's grin was ironic. "Somebody stabbed Munoz. D'you think he'd let Juanita get close enough to stick a shiv into him?"

"Ramon Toy, then?"

The slim man shook his head. "He couldn't have. He was wrestling with me at the time Munoz got his."

Matthews' eyes turned to Shackleford questioningly. The old man hurriedly struggled upright. "I assure you—"

"No, it wasn't Phineas," Hunter said. "He couldn't get that close, either. It must have been those others—Juanita's partners."

181

"They were afraid Munoz might buy it from . . . *her,* is that it?"

"What else? They knew she might simply be planning to sell the thing to the highest bidder."

"It seems to fit," Matthews agreed. He turned the full impact of his gaze on Hunter. "And now—one last question: You let her get away with that silver skull, Mr. Hunter, even though you knew its full significance. Why?"

Hunter turned his eyes away. It was the question he'd been asking himself all morning. Asking it, but unable to face up to the answer. Now that another had voiced it, he found himself genuinely embarrassed.

He said nothing. For once, the volatile hands were strangely still.

But the big man from the State Department refused to accept the silence. Inexorably, he ground on. "You'd been told—and you knew it to be true—that you were acting against your country." His voice became scornful. "And you didn't even enjoy the profits of betrayal."

"She saved my life, didn't she?" Hunter spoke softly, but savagely. "When Ramon was set to blast my guts, she chopped him down, didn't she? Her own brother. Could I turn her in after that? Doesn't that deserve something?"

But he could not lift his head to face the big man. He could feel the other's eyes seeking his, but he had to avoid the searching gaze.

Yet there was no avoiding what Matthews had to say. Quietly, his voice dripping acid, the man from the State Department said, "You expect me to believe that, Mr. Hunter? If she saved your life, you had saved hers only the night before. When her partners were torturing her. They canceled each other out. You didn't owe her a thing, Mr. Hunter, least of all the betrayal of your country."

As though beaten down by the contempt of the big man, Hunter's head sank lower and lower. The sensitive hands clasped themselves deep into his lap, shrinking from the castigation.

From deep in the chair, Shackleford chuckled softly. "She bamboozled him," the old man said. "She made him love her and then she bamboozled him."

Hunter's head jerked erect. As if Shackleford's remark had been a fist in his face.

"No!" He spat the word out.

The vehemence shocked them. Like a man breaking a trap, Hunter stood up. "I want to know one thing. Did she get away?"

Matthews faced him. "I'll tell you nothing."

Their eyes met. After a moment, Hunter's shoulders slumped. The other held the whip hand.

"It doesn't make any difference any more, does it?" he asked wearily. "If she got away, fine. If she didn't, she's beyond my help, isn't she?"

"No," Matthews said, "you can't help her any more."

Hunter sighed. "All right, then—here's the pitch. The idol she turned over to Moretti is a phoney."

"A phoney!" Shackleford's thin, twisted body stiffened sharply.

The man from the State Department said nothing. His eyes never left Hunter's face.

"That's right. A cheap imitation."

"But where . . . how . . .?" The old man was actually sputtering.

"It was the big thing down there, wasn't it? There must be copies in every home. Good luck charms. The way people keep saints in their homes up here. She brought one along just in case she'd need it to throw someone off the scent."

"But anyone would know—"

"Not Moretti. At least, that's the way I hoped it would work out."

"Just a minute, Mr. Hunter," Matthews cut in sharply. "You mean that Miss . . . Toy did not turn over *la calavera de plata* to Moretti, but an imitation."

"That's what I said."

Shackleford would not be silenced. His black eyes burned brightly. "Then Moretti actually got nothing for his twenty-five thousand dollars."

"Exactly nothing."

The old man thought a moment. "When he discovers he's been deluded, he'll go looking for revenge. Miss Toy is gone. The only one left is yourself."

Hunter said nothing.

The old man shook his head wonderingly. "Mr. Hunter," he said incredulously, "you're even more of a fool than I thought you were. You are actually risking your life—while letting her escape with the full profit . . ."

"I guess it adds up that way."

"And you will still have to handle Moretti—*alone.*"

Again, Hunter remained silent.

Unbelievingly, the bright black eyes measured him. "Foolish," he murmured. The bright black eyes softened.

The harsh voice sank until it was almost as if he were talking to himself. He repeated the word: "Foolish."

The look on his face became fond, almost paternal. "Foolish, but grandly so," he admitted admiringly. "I commend you for it—a magnificent gesture."

His hand went to Hunter's shoulder. "But take my advice, sir." He leaned forward to add earnestness to his words.

The intensity of his manner drew Hunter's gaze like a magnet.

"Mr. Hunter, get out—before Mr. Moretti comes back for his accounting!"

18

THEY WERE WAITING again, the three of them . . .

This time, it was for the report from Matthews' men. And, when the telephone rang, the big man from the State Department literally snatched the instrument from its cradle. He listened intently, asked a series of short incisive questions. Finally, satisfied, he hung up.

"It was just where you told us it would be," he said to Hunter. "In one of those ten-cent lockers at Penn Station." He shook his head wonderingly. "Though how you could risk leaving it in a place like that . . ."

Hunter said nothing. Fatigue had drained the last remaining vestiges of his strength. He sat slumped in the gray chair now, shoulders bent, head bowed, eyes fixed on immobile hands.

Matthews said: "I suppose I ought to thank you." He stopped then, realizing how ungracious the words sounded, went on to say, "Well, I do thank you, Mr. Hunter. Although your methods were hardly orthodox, they were effective."

Slowly, Hunter raised tortured eyes. "Goddam you, Matthews, you've got your stinking skull, haven't you?

186

Now, for God's sake—*what happened to that girl?*"

The big man's face lost its impassivity, softened into a look of pity.

"She's dead?" Hunter asked the questions as if he knew the answer.

"I'm sorry." Matthews turned his face away. "I guess they knew she'd try to double-cross them. They expect it of everyone—"

"How? How did it happen?"

"We don't know. We found them both, she and Moretti, outside the bank. Shot down in the middle of the street."

"Shot down!" The words were a groan from the depths of his being. "Dead!"

"The skull was gone. She still had the twenty-five thousand dollars in her purse. They must have just grabbed the idol and run."

"Dead!"

"I'm sorry."

The vibrant hands covered Hunter's face. His slumped body seemed, almost imperceptibly, to rock in a mourning motion.

The big man seemed, for once, at a loss for words. His eyes went down to the stricken form, then swept the walls of the room. Momentarily, they rested on Phineas Shackleford. The old man jerked his head toward the door.

Matthews sighed helplessly. He drew a deep breath. Finally, he said: "I'm afraid I'll have to leave now. Thanks again." The words sounded lame. "For the skull, I mean." He went to the door, turned to look back. Hunter hadn't moved. Matthews went out, closing the door softly behind him.

At his departure, Phineas Shackleford got up and approached the man in the chair.

"You threw away a million dollars, Mr. Hunter," the old man said quietly. "I admire you for it."

Hunter's hands buried themselves in his hair, tightened there.

The old man's voice was soothing, almost caressing. "At your age, I'd have done the same." There was something wistful in the way he said the words.

Wonderingly, Hunter raised his head.

The old man's eyes were tender. He lifted his hand to his face. "You find it hard to accept," he said, "that I was ever young, don't you?" There was a tremor in the bony fingers as they traced the wrinkles in the seamed, sunyellowed skin. His eyes were years away.

But he straightened abruptly. "You cost me a million dollars today, Mr. Hunter, and I repeat—I admire you for it, sir."

He smiled. "I bid you farewell, Mr. Hunter."

Fascinated, Peter Hunter watched the old man leave, then sat staring at the blank door. After a long minute, he rose and turned into the bedroom.

He stood in the doorway, leaned against the jamb. His eyes, shadowed now, swept the room. A momentary shudder crossed his face.

He stepped inside. The room was suffused with the vibrance of her. He swallowed hard.

He sat down on the bed. Her scent, faint and dry and provocative, still hung in the air.

A spot of color on the dresser caught his eye. He went to it, picked the object up.

It was the yellow claim check, the worthless yellow claim check she had left behind. His hands tightened as he stared down at it.

He whispered softly, to himself: *"La calavera de plata."*

And slowly, deliberately, he tore the worthless yellow claim check into a thousand tiny pieces.

THE END